KT-243-927

THE DISCIPLINE

THE DISCIPLINE

Marina Anderson

www.xratedbooks.co.uk

An *X Libris* Book

First published in Great Britain in 2002
by X Libris

Copyright © Marina Anderson 2002

The moral right of the author has been asserted.

*All characters in this publication are fictitious
and any resemblance to real persons, living or dead,
is purely coincidental.*

All rights reserved.
No part of this publication may be reproduced,
stored in a retrieval system, or transmitted, in any
form or by any means, without the prior
permission in writing of the publisher, nor be
otherwise circulated in any form of binding or
cover other than that in which it is published and
without a similar condition including this
condition being imposed on the subsequent purchaser.

A CIP catalogue record for this book
is available from the British Library.

ISBN 0 7515 3239 8

Typeset in Palatino by M Rules
Printed and bound in Great Britain by
Clays Ltd, St Ives plc

X Libris
An imprint of
Time Warner Books UK
Brettenham House
Lancaster Place
London WC2E 7EN

For Ellenie, with many thanks for all her help!

CHAPTER

1

The heavy wooden shutters of the old colonial-style house in the southern part of Rio de Janeiro were closed against the heat of the early-afternoon sun. It looked peaceful, an oasis of calm in the middle of the noisy, bustling, crowded streets.

In the large master bedroom of the house the atmosphere was far from peaceful. As an old-fashioned ceiling fan turned slowly and sluggishly, a tall, bronzed young woman lay spreadeagled in the middle of the vast bed. One of the thin shoulder straps of her red-and-white polka-dot dress had slipped down her arm, the skirt was bunched up round her waist and her right hand was working busily between her slender thighs

A man stood at the foot of the bed, watching and listening intently as she began to approach her climax. As her breathing grew ragged and her fingers moved more quickly he spoke. 'Slower, it's too soon. I want to watch you wait a little longer.'

The young woman groaned, moving restlessly against the mound of pillows beneath her head. Her waist-length blond hair was dark with sweat, and her hips twitched with desperate desire.

Although the man's voice was quiet, she knew him too well to disobey. She could feel the heat spreading upwards through her body, and her belly felt tight with need, but she forced herself to slow her fingers down, and moaned softly as the first deliciously exciting sparks of orgasm faded into the background.

The man nodded approvingly and smiled to himself as his blond mistress tentatively began to caress her breasts and belly in an effort to delay her climax. 'I didn't say begin all over again,' he remarked. 'Keep your hand between your thighs.'

'I shall come!' she protested.

'I doubt it.'

They both knew that he was right, and for another five minutes the beautiful bronzed body heaved and struggled to subdue the pleasure that was threatening to consume it. Finally, when she began to plead for release from her torment, the man moved.

Sitting on the side of the bed, he pulled the girl on to his lap, and she gasped as she felt herself impaled on his long, rigid erection. Realising that her body was finally going to be allowed release from the incredible sexual tension of the past hour, she wrapped her arms around the man's neck as he started to move her up and down with his hands.

At last the wonderful, scorching heat began to flood through her again, and she cried out with excitement, but then her rhythm was broken as the man stood up. Quickly she wrapped her legs around his waist, pressing herself against him as she tried to find the stimulation that she needed to climax.

The man was breathing rapidly, his excitement growing as he carried her across the room until her back was against the wall. Now he began thrusting in and out of her with increasing force, and she could see his startlingly blue eyes darken with passion and desire as they both approached their climax.

The blond girl knew the rules, but to her horror she suddenly realised that she wasn't going to be able to keep to them. He was moving too well, and had kept her on the edge for too long. She was going to come, before he'd been inside her for as long as he liked.

The man also realised it, and all at once the light went out of his eyes. 'No, Livia,' he cautioned her, but it was too late. She felt as though an electric current was surging through her body; all her muscles went rigid and then her belly went into violent spasms of almost painful pleasure, and she screamed with a mixture of ecstasy and fear.

As soon as her vagina contracted around him, the man's pleasure started to swamp him as well. A pulse jumped in the side of his neck as he tried to delay it, but it was no use. With a muffled groan he thrust one final time, grinding his hips against her as hard as he could, extracting every last bit of pleasure from the moment.

For a few seconds they remained locked together, the sweat on their bodies making it difficult for them to part, but then the man withdrew, and with an exclamation of annoyance he let the blonde fall to the ground in a tangled heap of tanned limbs and flowing hair.

She watched him from beneath lowered lids, wondering how he would react to her failure. To her surprise he didn't speak again, but instead went for a shower, then dressed and started to leave the room.

'I'm sorry, Carlos,' she said quickly. 'It was all too much for me. I . . .'

He turned to look at her, and there was an expression on his face that she'd never seen there before. He looked bored. 'I'm beginning to think that I'm wasting my time with you,' he remarked. 'You don't seem to understand the meaning of the word discipline.'

'How can you say that? When did I last fail you?' she asked.

'The point is that after all this time, I don't expect you to fail me at all. How can I rely on you to help me teach someone else discipline if you haven't mastered it yourself?'

The blonde's dark brown eyes widened in surprise. 'What do you mean, someone else?'

'I need a new hobby, a diversion. I thought that together we might introduce a newcomer to the kind of pleasures we enjoy.'

'Who?'

He shrugged. 'I have no idea yet. Someone will come along. I trust in fate.' With that he walked out of the door.

Once she was alone, Livia got up off the floor, padded over to the window, opened the shutters a little and looked at the city spread out below them.

Sometimes she wondered how she'd ever got herself involved with Carlos. She was young, rich and beautiful. Almost every man who saw her desired her, and yet here she was caught in the net of a man who'd taught her more than she'd ever wanted to know about herself. A man whose public persona was so at odds with his darkly perverse private life that no one would believe the truth about him, even if she ever dared to tell it.

The worst of it was that she was enthralled by him. She lived for the forbidden things that they did, the strange world of punishments and rewards that accompanied the sexual discipline which he expected his women to follow. He demanded much of her, but the rewards were great, and just the memory of the way he would sometimes touch her, or bind her, was enough to make her nipples harden with excitement.

4

Lost in her thoughts, it was several moments before she realised what was happening in the garden beneath the bedroom window. Someone was coming slowly up the long drive. It looked like a woman, but her clothes were strange. Not bright and casual, as most Brazilian women's clothes were, but dull. The dress looked to have long sleeves.

Opening the shutters wide, Livia leant out to get a better look. As she did so, the figure looked up, and it was then that Livia realised Carlos was being visited by a young nun. Hastily suppressing a giggle, she quickly closed the shutters again, deciding that after she'd showered she'd try and find out exactly what her lover had meant by his last remark.

Livia stepped beneath the powerful spray of water just as Chloe Reynolds, a novice nun in the first year of her novitiate, raised the brass knocker on the front door and banged loudly with it.

When she stepped into the delightfully cool hall, it was probably fortunate that she had no way of knowing that she was also taking her first steps into a very different world from the cloistered safety of the order of St Luke of the Holy Cross.

CHAPTER

2

Never in her entire life had Chloe seen a hallway like the one she was standing in now. The intricate marble tiles beneath her feet must have cost a small fortune, she thought to herself, and every exquisite object on the dark mahogany side tables looked like a collector's dream.

Although she hadn't wanted to come here, and if Sister Agatha hadn't had a migraine she certainly wouldn't have had to come alone, she was glad now that she'd been sent. She'd felt awkward walking through the front garden, listening to the shrieks of the peacocks, but now she was angry. Angry that in a country where there was so much poverty, people's consciences let them live like this.

Lost in her thoughts, she didn't hear Carlos Rocca's footsteps on the stairs. It wasn't until he gave a slight cough that she lifted her eyes from contemplating the floor tiles. But when she saw him, she found it almost impossible to breathe. It was as though the close, humid air outside had followed her in and was threatening to choke her.

'I was expecting Sister Agatha,' he said, his voice deep and surprisingly gentle. 'Unless she's suddenly lost forty years, I take it I misunderstood the message.'

Chloe struggled to speak. Not only did her chest feel tight, she was also giddy. It was a most peculiar sensation, and she didn't like it one bit. 'Sister Agatha has a migraine,' she explained, relieved to find that her voice sounded normal, except for a slight tremor. 'I was to have accompanied her, but because everyone else is so busy, I had to come alone.'

He gave a slight smile. 'I'm surprised they weren't concerned for your welfare.'

'You're well known to them. They said that you've given us assistance before.'

'Sister Agatha hardly offers a man the kind of temptation that you do, Sister . . . ?'

Heat suffused Chloe's cheeks and she felt herself start to tremble. She couldn't believe that a religious man, and a philanthropist, would speak to a nun in such a way. 'My name's Chloe,' she whispered, wishing he'd stop looking at her so intently with his deep blue eyes.

'Sister Chloe? That doesn't sound a very religious name!'

'We're allowed to keep our birth names if we want to these days. At the moment I'm only in the first year of my novitiate, which means that I don't have to choose my name for another twelve months. I don't suppose I will keep Chloe,' she added regretfully. 'You're right, it doesn't sound religious enough.'

Carlos gestured towards one of the heavy panelled doors in the hallway. 'Come through to my study. We'll talk there.'

Chloe hesitated for a moment, intimidated by the masculinity of his muscular body and his intense, almost pagan, charisma. Then she reminded herself that she was here for the children, and should have put such silliness behind her long ago. The fact that the man was tall, dark and handsome meant nothing to her now, just as she meant nothing to him. Her religion protected her. She wondered why she didn't feel more grateful.

As Carlos sat down behind his desk and surveyed the young novice sitting opposite him, he wondered how he was managing to keep his intense desire for her hidden. At last, just as he was beginning to question whether any woman would ever fascinate him again, this girl had been sent to him. She was literally a gift from heaven, he thought to himself with an inward laugh. Now he had to work out how to set about seducing her away from the convent and into his world.

'I take it you've come about a donation,' he remarked.

Chloe nodded. 'It's for the Brazilian street children. Over five hundred of them have already been killed by your own policemen this year, and—'

'They're not *my* policemen, Sister.'

'Of course not, I didn't mean . . . It's only that I'm from England and . . .'

Carlos leant forward, his eyes fixed on hers. 'What on earth is an English girl, and a novice nun at that, doing here in Brazil, walking around dangerous streets on her own, asking strange men for money?'

She looked flustered, which was what he'd intended. 'The streets aren't dangerous for me. My clothes mean that I'm safe. As for asking strange men for money, you've given to us before. You're one of our benefactors.'

'Giving money to worthy causes isn't necessarily the mark of a good man,' he said with a laugh. 'Perhaps it's how I atone for all my sins. You still haven't told me what you're doing so far from home.'

'I'm trying to reach inner freedom through the discipline of religion,' explained Chloe, hoping that he wouldn't laugh at her. 'The trouble is, I need to be doing things. I'm not very good at just praying and meditating. The order that I joined in England felt that if I came here and joined a working order, it would help me decide if this was truly my vocation.'

'And have you decided?'

'Not yet,' she confessed. 'But at least I'm making a difference. I don't suppose someone like you has any idea what it's like in the shanty towns, but the poverty is appalling. People live—'

Carlos held up his right hand. 'I don't need a lecture. Here, let me write you a cheque.' Opening his chequebook, he scribbled swiftly for a few seconds, tore off the cheque and handed it to her. 'Here, take it. If you think it will be used to help the poor, then I'm happy for you.'

He saw her startled expression as she looked at the figure on the cheque. 'Of course it will help them!' she exclaimed. 'It's far too much. I never expected . . .'

He looked intently at her. 'No amount of money can save your street children, or the poor. Before you come back to me for more, I want you to promise to do something for me.'

'Anything,' she said quickly. 'You've been so generous.'

'Do some investigating. Find out for yourself where the money goes. I think you'll soon realise that more of it is used in bribes than ever reaches the needy. This is a corrupt city, Sister Chloe. Most people here lack the discipline you seem so anxious to acquire.'

He watched her fingers tighten round the cheque, and then she stood up and walked towards the door, clearly anxious to get away from him. 'I'm sorry that you have such a jaundiced view of the world,' she retorted. 'I shall pray for you.'

For a moment he almost felt sorry for her, but then he hardened his heart. It was best that she knew the truth. Best for her, and definitely best for him. Moving quickly across the room, he managed to open the door before she reached it, and then watched her walk towards him.

Her knee-length grey skirt revealed perfect black-stockinged legs, and her short black veil, with the narrow mauve band of the novice, showed a glimpse of dark curly hair beneath it The outfit was far more seductive than any low-cut dress, and he felt himself harden with desire. Somehow he had to have her. Had to teach her his own kind of discipline. He had the feeling she'd be an excellent pupil.

'Don't forget to do your research,' he reminded her as he held the front door open. She didn't reply, but he saw her almond-shaped grey eyes flick upwards and saw too the expression of pitying contempt in them. It didn't matter. She'd soon learn the truth, and then she'd be back because she wouldn't know where else to go.

Chloe walked as quickly as was considered proper down the long path, and licked at her dry lips with the tip of her tongue. Now that she was out of the house, and away from the disturbing presence of Carlos Rocca, it was easier for her to breathe. She'd never had a man stare so intently at her before, as though he could see right into her soul.

Although his cheque was amazingly generous, he obviously wasn't a good man. To suggest that the money being raised in the city was used to bribe people was despicable. All the same, she'd check up on it, see for herself exactly where it all went.

Unfortunately, it wasn't just his allegations that had disturbed her. Even after she got back to the ramshackle building that served as the headquarters for the order, she kept remembering the contrast between his blue eyes and his tanned skin, and the way his wavy brown hair had curled up on the edge of his collar at the nape of his neck.

It was unforgivable, but she didn't confess any of it, because deep down she knew that she wasn't sorry. It was a frightening thing to discover about herself.

CHAPTER

3

Carlos settled himself comfortably in the depths of the soft-cushioned chair, watching intently as Livia and a Brazilian girlfriend writhed together on a rug on the floor in front of him.

The girl, Juanita, had been to the house before. She was the daughter of one of the city's most infamous drug barons, but Carlos had nothing to fear. His power was the greater, and the man knew it. He believed that her visits were an honour, a sign that Carlos would support him if any of his rivals tried to remove him. In this he was completely wrong. All that interested Carlos was the pleasure Juanita gave him, and that he and Livia gave the girl.

Tonight was particularly exciting, because Juanita had been told that she must remain silent the entire time. Normally she would murmur incoherently as her pleasure mounted, and then scream in ecstasy when she climaxed. Although used to playing different games on every visit, she was finding tonight a struggle. As a result, it was difficult for Carlos to wait his turn.

Livia's blond hair was spread out over Juanita's stomach, and as she moved her head between her friend's thighs, the long strands tickled the sensitive flesh of the

other girl's belly. This gentle stimulation, coupled with the soft, sweeping movements of Livia's knowing tongue, was driving the girl to distraction.

When Juanita's head began to move from side to side, and her large nipples were rigid, Carlos got up from his chair and stood looking down at the two of them. His own breathing was rapid, his chest rising and falling beneath his open-necked cream shirt, and Juanita's huge, liquid brown eyes stared up at him imploringly as she tried to remain silent.

Carlos swallowed hard. This was how he wanted to see the novice nun, Chloe, who'd come to the house two weeks earlier. This was the kind of discipline he wanted her to learn. He could imagine how she'd look in this situation, her newly awakened body struggling to subdue itself in order to please him.

Aware that her lover was looking down on them, Livia's tongue moved more carefully over Juanita's swollen clitoris. She knew what Carlos really wanted. He wanted Juanita to fail, and he expected Livia to make certain this happened. If it didn't, if Juanita managed to remain silent, then it would be Livia who was punished.

Although his punishments always ended in pleasure, this was something she wanted to avoid tonight. She wanted to see Juanita squirming and crying out as her body was tormented and teased for her failure. She wanted to take part in administering the punishment, and so she had to make Juanita fail.

The other girl's thighs were trembling, and when Livia flicked her tongue inside Juanita she felt her hips rise up from the floor as her body tried to reach orgasm. Hastily Livia moved her mouth, and heard Juanita's breath catch in her throat with disappointment.

13

Now Livia moved herself up, until her body was covering Juanita's, and moved around on the smooth, silken flesh, pressing her hips hard against Juanita's while at the same time cupping her swollen vulva with one hand. Her fingers kept up a firm, steady pressure and she could imagine the sweet ache that Juanita must be experiencing.

As she bent her head and started to draw one of the tight nipples into her mouth, Juanita stared frantically at her, shaking her head despairingly. Livia smiled at her, knowing that the longer she delayed that final moment of hot, flooding release, the greater the chances were that Juanita would moan or cry out. Soon, very soon, she would fail.

Juanita was in despair. She loved coming to Carlos Rocca's house and lived for the incredible sensual pleasure that he and Livia gave her, but at the same time she was a little afraid of him. She'd only failed to obey him once before, but she remembered all too well what had happened then, and she didn't want it to happen again.

When Livia's soft mouth closed around her aching right nipple, she felt a groan rising in her throat, and gulped down air in an effort to keep the sound away. She was so close to coming. Between her thighs her flesh was throbbing and burning, while her hips were jerking as though they had a life of their own.

The first tantalising flashes of red-hot pleasure had already darted through her, but Livia knew what she was doing, and kept stopping the stimulation before Juanita could climax. Even now, as she sucked on the needy nipple, her hand was pressing against the source of Juanita's pleasure with a firm, even pressure that excited without satisfying.

Slowly, very slowly, Livia slid down Juanita's body, until her head was once more between her thighs. As her slim fingers carefully opened her up, Juanita gasped and immediately Carlos moved closer, his blue eyes watching her intently. She wanted to keep silent, wanted to obey him, but knew that it was going to be impossible.

When Livia's lips closed around her clitoris and began to suck gently on it, Juanita gave up. She felt the heat spreading through her, felt her muscles tighten and her body jerk, and then her orgasm came crashing down on her. It was sharper, more intense than any she'd experienced before, and as she opened her mouth to cry out with delight at the unimaginable pleasure of it, she saw Carlos give a tiny smile of amused satisfaction.

The contractions of her climax went on and on, and Juanita heard herself moaning and shouting, but she couldn't help it. It was all so good, and for a brief moment she didn't care what happened afterwards, because her lush, supple body was made for this kind of pleasure.

Listening to Juanita's cries of passion, Carlos wondered what Chloe would sound like in the throes of sexual excitement. He doubted if she'd be as abandoned as the Brazilian girl, but that would only make her more of a challenge.

When Juanita was finally silent, she lay looking up at him with a mixture of anxiety and desire. Livia was watching him too, and he nodded briefly at her as a sign of his pleasure. She'd done well, but then she was always good at games that involved other women.

'I don't think you were silent, do you, Juanita?' he asked. She shook her head.

'A pity, you were doing well until the end. Come with me. It's time for your forfeit.'

He held out his hand, and Juanita took it reluctantly. Passively, she let him lead her through into an adjoining room. Livia followed, closing the door behind the three of them, and then stood waiting to see what would happen.

Carlos gestured towards the bow window, which had a wide seat in the bay. 'Stand over there, face out of the window and put your hands on the seat,' he ordered Juanita. As she slowly moved to obey him, he drew a glass jar out of one of the bureau drawers and dipped his fingers into the cream inside it.

Juanita glanced back over her shoulder, and immediately tried to spin round, but Carlos was too quick for her and pushed her back into position. 'You know how good this can be if you only relax,' he reminded her.

The Brazilian girl's body trembled, but Carlos knew he was right. He loved to take her this way, thrusting into her second, tighter entrance and feeling her initial resistance weaken as the discomfort turned into a dark, forbidden pleasure.

Livia sat on the seat next to her friend, and while Carlos began to cover his tight erection with the lubricating cream, she started to gently caress Juanita between her thighs. She slid her fingers up and down the channel between her inner sex lips, and when Juanita's juices started to flow she nodded at Carlos.

By now he was painfully hard, and grasping the Brazilian girl round her waist he eased himself inside her, rotating his hips so that he was touching every possible nerve ending inside her sensitive back passage. She tightened herself against him, trying to expel him, but he only grasped her more firmly still. When she whimpered, he whispered in her ear, reminding her of what was to come.

At first she twisted and struggled, trying to resist him. Then, after a few moments, he felt her relax as sweet pleasure began to take over. Now Livia removed her hand, leaving Carlos free to reach round Juanita until it was his fingers that were playing with her.

He started to move himself rhythmically in and out,

gently at first but then harder as he imagined that it was Chloe he was inside. In his mind it was Chloe who was moaning and sobbing, ashamed of her own dark sexuality. It was Chloe's clitoris that he was pinching between his finger and thumb, and it was Chloe that he emptied himself into as he came in an explosive climax that left him feeling weak and drained.

He scarcely heard Juanita's screams of shamed gratitude, or noticed the strange look that Livia gave him as he withdrew from her friend, because his thoughts were elsewhere. To him this had been nothing more than a practice run, albeit a very enjoyable one.

One day, no matter how long he had to wait, his dream would come true, and if Chloe put up more resistance than Juanita, then so much the better. Running his hand down the Brazilian girl's moist back, he left the two young women alone together, showered and went to bed.

If his spies were right, then his disillusioned little nun was already on her way back to England. He'd expected her to run to him for help, but clearly she was more independent than he'd thought, which should only increase the pleasure of the chase. Although she didn't know it, he and Livia would soon be joining her in England too.

CHAPTER

4

A s Chloe sorted through the plastic bags of clothes, toys and household knick-knacks that were the result of their most recent street collection, she couldn't help comparing the damp drizzle of an English day in June with the sun-drenched heat of Copacabana beach.

She'd been back in England for six weeks, and was still struggling to come to terms with all that had happened to her since her fateful meeting with Carlos Rocca. There were times when she wished she'd never set eyes on the man, because he'd brought her world crashing down round her ears and made it impossible for her to stay in Brazil.

Although she'd been lucky enough to land a job as a paid member of a London-based charity for Brazilian street children, the money was so poor that the only room she could afford was little better than the tiny cell-like room containing just a single bed that she'd lived in while in Rio.

She worked long hours, often staying on after everyone else had gone, because there was nothing else in her life. Everything that she'd believed in was gone, and she wasn't getting the satisfaction from her work that she'd expected. Every day, in fact almost every hour, she'd find her thoughts wandering to her first glimpse of Carlos in the hallway of his magnificent house, and she couldn't understand why.

She'd met a lot of handsome men when she was younger, before she'd decided to embrace the religious life, and none of them had affected her in the same way. It was as though his strange dark-blue, black-lashed eyes held a sense of danger, which ignited something in her, something new and disturbing.

It was only at night, when she couldn't control her thoughts, that her subconscious mind let her see what this might involve. When she woke from these dreams she was drenched in sweat, and would quickly pray for guidance. However, she was beginning to suspect that she may have been using religion to protect herself from an inner darkness that she was afraid to confront.

'There you are!' said Lizzie, the branch organiser, as she entered the room. 'I hoped I'd find you here. I've got a job for you. Something different for once. We've had a letter from a man living in London who was born in Brazil. He's very interested in our work and wants someone to go round and talk to him about it in detail before he decides whether or not to give a regular donation. It sounds as though it would be a lot of money if he did choose in our favour, so make sure you do a good job on him!'

'But I'm new,' protested Chloe. 'You should go yourself – or send Anna. She's the sophisticated kind of woman who'd appeal to a wealthy, ageing Brazilian.'

'He might be young for all I know. Anyway, I can't send Anna. He's asked to see you.'

'Me?' Chloe stared incredulously at her. 'That's impossible. I don't know anyone in London.'

'Well, apparently someone knows you. He said he met you once when you were living in Rio de Janeiro.'

Chloe's mouth went dry. 'I can't go,' she said quickly.

19

'I'm out of practice at making conversation. It's going to take me months before I can socialise again, you know that. I'll do anything else – address all the envelopes, do cold telephone calling – anything but . . .'

Lizzie laughed. 'There's no need to panic. You're very good at explaining our work to people. Let's face it, you're the only one of us who's been there and knows what it's really like. Besides, as you've decided you want to rejoin the world again, you've got to start some time, and this is a golden opportunity. He lives in a nice area, very posh.'

Chloe's stomach felt peculiar, as though it were getting tied up in a knot. 'I really don't want to do this, Lizzie,' she said quietly.

'It's all in a good cause,' retorted Lizzie briskly. 'I've arranged for you to go there at three this afternoon. I thought three sounded a very civilised hour. You might get tea and scones!'

Chloe knew when she was beaten. 'All right,' she agreed miserably.

'Cheer up. He might be young, handsome and single as well as rich, then you'll thank me! His name's Carlos Rocca, by the way. Ring any bells?'

Chloe shook her head She'd already known, of course, but the last thing she wanted was to start discussing her previous meeting with Carlos, and the part he'd played in her decision to leave the order. Also, if he'd taken the trouble to look her up while he was in London, then she very much doubted that she'd have any reason to thank Lizzie.

At precisely three o'clock that afternoon, she rang the bell of the three-storey house in Maida Vale. She hadn't known what to wear for the meeting. Most of her clothes had been given away when she'd become a postulant a year earlier, and those that she'd kept were too loose, because she'd lost a lot of weight in Brazil – a combination of the heat and the nuns' poor diet.

In the end she'd picked the best cotton dress she owned, a simple gold-coloured shift, and decided to ignore the fact that it was a cool, wet day. The last thing she wanted was to look like some kind of pathetic waif when she faced the man again.

A middle-aged woman opened the front door and looked questioningly at her. 'Yes?'

'I'm Sister Chloe, and I've come to see Mr Rocca about the—'

The woman raised her eyebrows. '*Sister* Chloe?'

She wished the ground would open up and swallow her. 'No, sorry, of course not. That is, I used to be a sister – well, a nun – but of course I'm not any more, which is why I'm wearing this dress. I . . .'

She was spared further embarrassment by the appearance of Carlos himself. 'It's all right, Mrs Clarke, I was expecting the young lady. She really was a nun once,' he added. 'I accept that's rather difficult to believe today, but I promise you it's true.'

As Chloe walked into the house, she wondered if the dress had been such a good idea after all. His eyes had lingered on her for a very long time while he was talking to his house-keeper, and even now she was certain that he was watching her closely as he followed her down the entrance hall.

After he'd shown her into a small, beautifully furnished drawing room, he sat down on a white leather armchair and looked approvingly at her. 'A great improvement,' he murmured. 'Although there was something very seductive about the black veil.'

'Our branch organiser said that you'd asked to talk to me about the charity,' said Chloe, trying to ignore the way he was studying her. 'She said that you needed to have more information before deciding whether to support us or not. I admit I find that a little strange, considering the fact that you gave us a large donation in Rio, but perhaps you're going to tell me that the people I'm working with now are corrupt too.'

'I take it from that remark that you did the research I suggested?'

'Yes.'

'And discovered that I was right?'

'If you hadn't been right, I'd still be there, completing my novitiate.' It was difficult to keep the bitterness out of her voice.

Carlos's eyes narrowed. 'I hope you're not blaming me for the corruption you uncovered?'

'No, that would be very unreasonable of me.'

He nodded. 'It would, but I think that you do. Tell me, do you really miss being a nun?'

'Of course I do. It was my life! Now it's all been taken away from me, and I don't know what to do.'

'A charity worker is a very worthy thing to be.'

Chloe was certain she could detect a note of mockery in his voice. 'You make that sound like an insult.'

'Then I apologise. It's only that you seem to me to be a girl who is running away from herself, trying to conceal the truth from everyone. Why is this? Are you ashamed of what you're really like?'

'Of course not! Why should I be?'

'That is what intrigues me. I'll ring for some tea, and then we'll talk a little more.'

Chloe watched him get up and pull on a tasselled cord that hung next to the fireplace. He was wearing a dark suit with a white shirt and a blue-and-maroon tie. He looked exactly like the intelligent, sophisticated industrialist he was known to be in his own country, and yet there was something wrong. Beneath the smooth veneer, she sensed something primitive; something dangerous, that could occasionally be glimpsed in the depths of his eyes. It was this that she had remembered, and to her shame, something inside her responded to it.

After Mrs Clarke had brought in a tray of tea and biscuits, Carlos gestured for Chloe to pour. 'You're right in thinking that I have all the information I need on your charity,' he remarked as she tried to keep the hand holding the teapot steady. 'I really wanted to see you again.'

Chloe looked directly at him. 'Why?'

'You interest me. I believe that we have more in common than you may think.'

'I doubt it,' she said hastily. 'We're from different worlds. You think I'm amusing and strange, that's all. You probably believe that everyone should want to live like you, but that's just vanity, I'm afraid.'

As soon as she'd spoken she knew that she'd gone too far. She'd insulted a possible patron, but it was too late to call the words back. Glancing at him, she was unable to tell his reaction because the expression on his face was completely neutral, almost indifferent.

'Are you afraid to find out if what I'm saying is true?' he enquired softly.

'I know it isn't true.'

'Then come out to dinner with me. We'll go for a meal, and talk some more. It may surprise you to know that I too believe in discipline and rules; it's simply a different kind of discipline from the one you originally chose to follow.'

'I don't think I want to come out to dinner with you,' said Chloe, knowing full well that she did.

'But you want me to give generously to your charity, don't you? Surely one harmless dinner isn't too high a price to pay?'

23

Chloe looked steadily at him. 'That sounds like blackmail.'

He nodded. 'It is blackmail.'

His honesty took her by surprise. 'That's disgusting!'

'It's the way the world goes round. Your time in Rio de Janeiro must have taught you that.'

'But this is London,' she protested. 'It's different here.'

'People are the same the world over. Here, in England, such things are hidden below the surface. In Brazil it's an accepted way of life. For myself, I prefer the Brazilian way. I dislike hypocrites. Now, will you come out to dinner with me or not?'

Chloe hesitated. She didn't have anything else to do. All her evenings were spent alone in her bedsit, with only the pigeons on the small balcony for company. Despite this, her instincts told her that she should refuse, even if it meant the charity losing a donation. This man was dangerous, and she wasn't naïve enough to think that he wanted only to talk to her.

She opened her mouth to refuse, then, abruptly tiring of playing safe, changed her mind. 'If you really want to take me out for a meal, it would be selfish of me to refuse,' she replied.

Carlos smiled. 'How altruistic of you to put the charity before your own feelings! I'll pick you up at eight o'clock tomorrow night. You must give me your address before you leave. I'm certain we'll have a very interesting evening.'

As she began to drink her tea, Chloe couldn't help wondering exactly what Carlos Rocca meant by interesting.

CHAPTER

5

'Where does the little nun live?' shouted Livia, as Carlos showered before going to pick up Chloe.

'On the other side of the river. A very poor address, which is to our advantage.'

Livia didn't reply. She wasn't completely happy with what Carlos had planned. Although the prospect of initiating a sexual novice into their world of disciplined eroticism was exciting, it carried a risk. It was the same risk that all his games carried when they involved another woman: he might prefer her to Livia.

Glancing at the bed, she saw that he'd laid out one of his best suits and his favourite Italian silk tie. Fear touched her, making her stomach tighten. He was a man who was easily bored, who moved in a world where all the women were sophisticated and highly sexed. An ex-nun, novice or otherwise, was certain to hold his interest for a time.

Quickly she slid open the glass doors of the shower cubicle, slipped off her dress and walked inside to join Carlos. He was standing with his back to her, but turned his head as she slid her arms round his waist, her fingers caressing his damp skin.

'I'm in a hurry,' he murmured.

'We've got time,' she responded, moving her mouth down his spine and kissing every vertebra.

For a second it seemed as though he wasn't going to respond, but then he turned to face her, his eyes bright with excitement. Grabbing hold of her, he twisted her round until she was standing with her back against the wall opposite the shower head. Now he caught hold of her hands, and pushed them up above her head, pinning them against the tiled surface as he bent his head and nipped lightly at each of her nipples in turn.

Livia began to squirm with excitement, and he quickly thrust a knee between her legs, pushing it upwards so that she could stimulate herself against it. 'Make yourself come like that,' he said hoarsely, and then his mouth was moving over her sensitive breasts again.

Livia's hips jerked as she rubbed her vulva against his leg, and she started to grow heavy and damp between her thighs. She could feel his tongue moving roughly over the soft underside of each of the swollen globes in turn. His breathing was quickening all the time, and as she felt herself tightening deep inside her belly, he lowered his leg and pushed his straining erection against her aroused entrance.

'Come now!' he commanded, pushing himself inside her, but she wasn't quite ready. He was demanding her obedience too soon, and she nearly cried out with frustration because she desperately wanted things to go well.

Aware that she wasn't ready, Carlos started to rotate his hips in tiny circles, trying to touch her G-spot, and at the same time he fastened his mouth over her left breast, sucked at it for a few seconds and then closed his teeth hard over the aching tip of the nipple.

As a delicious shard of red-hot pain lanced through her, Livia's body shuddered with delight and she climaxed at the same moment as her lover. When the last tremors had died away, Carlos gently pushed the damp hair back off her face and kissed her deeply on the mouth.

'Delectable!' he said with satisfaction. 'I wish our ex-nun had been watching.'

'She'd have been very shocked!' laughed Livia, running her fingers over her bruised nipple.

'Of course. I want to see her shocked,' he replied. Then he squeezed her sore nipple sharply between the finger and thumb of his right hand before leaving Livia alone in the shower.

Shivering at the wonderful, hot, dark pain that he'd deliberately caused, Livia felt desire rising in her again. That was the problem with Carlos. It was impossible to get enough of him.

'I think I've had enough to drink already,' said Chloe, as Carlos began to refill her glass.

'Nonsense, you've hardly had anything.'

'Well, just a little then.' Chloe wasn't used to drinking, but it seemed rude to refuse, and anyway the wine was delicious.

'So tell me the truth. Do you still regret deciding that you weren't cut out to be a nun'

Chloe couldn't remember when she'd last felt so relaxed, and she was sure that Carlos would understand what she was talking about if she was honest with him. 'I wasn't ever certain that I was cut out to be a nun,' she confessed. 'In a way I think I wanted to prove to myself that I could cope with the discipline it involved. My parents were always on the move. They let me grow up without any real boundaries or guidelines. Their only attempt at setting any kind of standard for me to follow was when they sent me to a convent school. It was one of the nuns who suggested that I should consider entering a religious order.'

She was aware that he was watching her closely. 'Was this because you were naturally very good?' he asked softly.

Chloe tried to suppress a giggle. 'Certainly not! Quite the opposite really, but according to Sister Clare, it's never the girls who think they want to be nuns who are really being called. I admit I found their interest quite flattering, which shows a rather vain and shallow nature!'

His next words were spoken so quietly that she had to lean over the table to hear him. 'Do you find it hard obeying rules?'

'Oh yes,' she said cheerfully, aware that she'd definitely drunk too much. She wasn't usually this open. 'When someone tells me what to do, my natural instinct is to do the opposite. Of course, I soon conquered that once I entered the convent.'

'Of course.'

'I still think I'd have made a good nun,' she continued. 'I was doing really well, but when I discovered what was happening to all the money we were collecting in Rio, I started to question everything. I mean, how could they justify paying out bribes to thugs and crooked policemen when small children were—'

'It was a question of survival. You know, I think I did you a favour. You definitely weren't cut out to be a nun.'

She felt a little giddy, and hoped he'd hurry up and order some coffee. 'Maybe not,' she agreed. 'I like my work at the charity.'

'Surely you don't like where you're living?' asked Carlos.

Chloe shook her head, and the room spun. 'No, of course not. It's horrid, but it's all I can afford.'

To her relief she saw Carlos turn and catch the waiter's eye. 'Two coffees, please. You know, Chloe, I might have the solution to your problem. There are three spare bedrooms in my London house. Why don't you use one of those?'

'I couldn't,' she said hastily. 'It wouldn't look right. I hardly know you, and—'

'I don't live there alone. Livia, my Brazilian girlfriend, has flown over with me. Drink your coffee and I'll show you round the house before I drive you home.'

'I don't understand why you want to help me,' muttered Chloe, wishing she could just curl up and go to sleep.

'Because I feel responsible for you. After all, if it hadn't been for me, you'd still be living in Rio de Janeiro with all your illusions intact.'

She was sure there was more to it than that, but the truth was she wanted to see the rest of his luxurious house, and she also wanted to be with him for a little longer. 'All right,' she agreed, 'as long as Livia's in tonight.'

'Oh yes,' Carlos assured her with a smile. 'Livia will be in, and she'll be very interested to meet you.'

By the time Carlos drew up outside his home, Chloe was asleep in the passenger seat. He glanced at her, her face illuminated by the light from a nearby street lamp. She looked unbelievably innocent, and his mouth was dry with excitement.

This was the difficult part, getting her to agree to live under the same roof as him. If he could accomplish that, then he was confident that the rest would be easy. He knew women, and could tell from the way Chloe moved, dressed, ate and drank that she was deeply sensual. All she needed was someone to show her the truth about herself. It might be a shock, but she'd get over it. In the end she'd be grateful to him, just as he was grateful to her now for bringing excitement back into his jaded life.

He stroked the side of her face, and her eyelids flew open. 'What's the matter?'

'Nothing. You fell asleep. This is where I live.'

'I'm sorry, it must have been the wine.'

He nodded. 'Very probably. Let's go in.'

Before they'd reached the front door, Livia opened it. She stood framed in the doorway, looking magnificent and sexy in a tight-fitting dark-red dress, with her blond hair falling to her shoulders. 'I've brought Chloe back to look over the house,' said Carlos. 'She's living in a horrible flat in Tooting at the moment. I thought she could use one of our spare bedrooms, since she works so near.'

'I didn't know we were taking in lodgers,' muttered Livia, as Carlos brushed past her with Chloe just behind him.

'It's for a good cause,' said Carlos, struggling not to sound as annoyed as he felt at Livia's interruption. 'Chloe works for a charity that's trying to help Brazilian street children, which, as you know, is a cause very close to my heart.'

Chloe stood blinking in the hall. 'I'd forgotten how lovely it is,' she said sleepily.

'I'd imagine it's quite a change to your present flat.'

'Sorry, I'm really tired and confused. Why do you want me to stay here?'

'Because you deserve a nicer place to live, nearer where you work, and I'm partly to blame for what's happened to you. Come on, follow me.'

He was counting on the fact that if he spoke with enough authority she'd obey him, and when she did he felt a buzz of excitement. Clearly her first instinct was still to follow instructions, just as she had as a nun. Now, as long as she accepted the offer of a room, her initiation into his world could begin.

Opening the door into the largest spare bedroom, he

stepped back to let her look in. The colour scheme was all soft browns and cream. The bed, dressing table and wardrobes were natural pine, and cut-glass vases full of green-and-white floral decorations were dotted around the room.

'It's beautiful,' whispered Chloe, 'and so restful. I could lie down and go to sleep here right now.'

Carlos glanced at Livia, who quickly took the younger girl by the arm. 'Why don't you?' she suggested with a smile. 'You're very tired. We can talk more in the morning.'

'I don't think I should. I . . .'

Livia steered Chloe towards the bed, and within seconds she was lying on her side on top of the covers, her head resting on her hands and her eyes closed.

Carlos studied her deep breathing and nodded with satisfaction. 'Out for the count!' he said to Livia, as they closed the door on her. 'This is all going exactly to plan. Now, here's what I want to happen in the morning . . .' As he continued to talk, Livia listened carefully, and by the time they went to bed, she was almost as excited as her lover.

When Chloe first opened her eyes, she couldn't think where she was. There was a little daylight coming through a crack between the curtains covering a window to the right of her bed, but nothing looked familiar. Then, slowly, she began to remember the night before.

Glancing at her watch, she saw that it was six o'clock. She was used to waking early, but this morning she had a feeling that a noise had woken her. Quietly she lay in her bed, listening.

After a few moments she knew that she was right. It sounded as though someone was sobbing or groaning somewhere in the house. The sound would continue for a minute or longer, and then there would be a long pause before it began again. She felt her pulse quicken, and slipping out of bed opened her bedroom door and stepped out on to the landing.

The noise was much louder there. It was a strange, keening kind of cry and she walked slowly along, trying to pinpoint exactly where it was coming from. Suddenly the noise grew much louder, and as she turned her head towards it, she found herself looking through an open bedroom door.

Livia was crouched on all fours on top of a large four-poster bed, and it was she who was making the noise that had disturbed Chloe's sleep. Her head was tipped back, her eyes half closed, and she was naked except for a thick leather collar round her neck. Attached to the collar was a thin leash.

Carlos was kneeling behind Livia, his right hand gripping the top of her right thigh and his left hand gripping the leash. He too was naked, his hips and belly pressed tightly against Livia's body. Every time he moved his hips back and forth, Livia groaned, and Chloe quickly realised that it was with pleasure.

Then, just as Livia's breath began to quicken and the tendons on her neck grew rigid, Carlos flicked the long leash beneath her, so that it struck the soft skin of her belly. Again she cried out, but to the watching Chloe, standing rooted to the spot, it seemed as though this time there was pain as well as pleasure in the sound.

'Please, please don't keep spoiling it,' cried Livia, as Carlos started to move in and out of her again.

'Sshh!' he whispered tenderly, and, to her shame, Chloe felt her nipples growing hard. 'Be good,' he murmured. 'Not much longer to wait now.'

He quickened his pace, and again Livia threw back her head. Carlos began moving his right hand under her, stroking her between her thighs. Her breathing grew even more ragged, and she started to shake. 'Yes! Yes!' she cried, and Chloe swallowed hard.

At that moment, Carlos looked directly over Livia's head, and his penetrating blue eyes met Chloe's. As he casually flicked the leash against the frantic Livia's breasts, causing her to cry out in protest once more, Chloe forced herself to move. Grabbing the door-handle, she slammed the door shut on the shocking scene and fled back to her bedroom.

CHAPTER

6

It was eight o'clock before Chloe ventured downstairs. She felt strange, excited but at the same time frightened by what she'd witnessed. She wasn't entirely ignorant about sex, and had even experienced some teenage fumblings in the backs of cars before she'd decided on her vocation. However, what she'd seen happening between Carlos and Livia was way beyond anything she'd imagined, and had left her deeply disturbed.

After she'd got back to her room, she hadn't been able to settle. Instead she'd moved restlessly around, and when she'd showered, her hands had lingered on her breasts and stroked her nipples until they hardened into small pink peaks.

Now all she wanted was to get back to the security of her room in Tooting, and the safe, if dull, routine of her daily life. Carlos Rocca had the ability to arouse dark, bizarre longings in her, leaving her afraid of herself.

'There you are!' exclaimed Carlos, hurrying down the stairs. Putting an arm gently round her waist, he led her through into a small dining room. 'You need some toast and coffee before we go and collect your things. I'm sure you must have a headache this morning!'

'A bit,' she admitted, which was the understatement of the year.

'I'm sorry, I forgot that you'd be unused to alcohol. The nuns weren't secret drinkers, I take it?'

'Of course not,' laughed Chloe. She was relieved that he hadn't mentioned what she'd seen earlier. When he'd looked directly at her, she'd been horrified, wondering how she could face him when they next met. It seemed that she needn't have worried. Clearly the entire incident was to be ignored.

'What do you mean, collect my things?' she asked as she sipped the coffee brought by the housekeeper.

He glanced at her in surprise. 'Well, as you're moving in here, I assume you'll want to fetch your clothes and any belongings you have in that dingy little room.'

Chloe stared at him. 'I haven't said that I'm moving in here, have I?'

'No, but I assumed . . .'

'I couldn't possibly impose myself on you and Livia. In any case, I can't afford to live here. Rooms like the one I slept in last night cost—'

He looked genuinely shocked. 'I wouldn't charge you for the room! As I said, I feel partly responsible for the situation you're in now. In addition, it's another way I can help your charity, by giving their best worker somewhere close at hand to live.'

'I had no idea you were such a charitable person,' said Chloe drily.

He nodded thoughtfully. 'You're cynical, and who can blame you? Believe me, I want to do this for you.'

'Why?' asked Chloe.

'I think you already know the answer to that,' he said softly. Then he reached out and stroked the side of her face lightly with the back of his left hand. 'Come and live with us,' he urged her. 'You're missing the discipline of your old life. Let me show you a different kind of discipline, where the reward is greater pleasure than you can begin to imagine.'

A vision of Livia, naked except for the leather collar, flashed through Chloe's mind. She looked deep into Carlos Rocca's eyes, and saw desire there. Desire and something else, something frightening yet at the same time thrilling. The room was heavy with erotic tension, she could hardly breathe, and when she tried to look away from him, she couldn't.

'I'm afraid,' she whispered.

He nodded. 'Of course you are, but you must trust me. Learn to live, Chloe. You've been shut away from the world for too long. My ways will suit you. There's nothing to fear except yourself.'

As he slowly traced the outline of her mouth with one finger, she closed her eyes and gave a tiny sigh of submission. From the moment they first met, this had always been her destiny, and now she felt brave enough to face it.

'Will you come and stay with me?' he repeated.

'Yes,' murmured Chloe. 'I want to learn your discipline.'

When she opened her eyes, he smiled at her and his normally impassive face looked younger and kinder for a moment. 'Good girl,' he said gently, and then he stood up and left the room.

'You got what you wanted then,' said Livia, sipping freshly squeezed orange juice as she stood looking out of the French windows at the back of the house.

'Naturally.'

'I can't imagine why you want her so badly. I'd have expected you to prefer someone more sophisticated. Once you've taken her virginity, what use will she be to you?'

'Her virginity is of little interest to me. I see it merely as an obstacle to the real delights that lie ahead.'

Livia's lip curled. 'She wanted to be a nun, Carlos, and now she's a charity worker! Your way of life isn't likely to interest her. She'll be terrified.'

'I don't think so. Our little ex-nun has more to her than you imagine.'

She tapped her fingers restlessly against the glass. 'I'm bored. I hate England. I hate the climate, I hate the food and I loathe the people. They're all dull. When are we going back to Rio?'

'Not for a long time. How is Felipe coming along?'

Livia's head turned sharply towards her lover. 'What do you mean?'

Carlos sighed. 'You should know by now that it's impossible to keep secrets from me. While I've been out, you've been amusing yourself by training Felipe. Is he a good pupil?'

The blood drained from Livia's face. 'It's only a game, something to cheer me up when you're busy. He doesn't mean anything to me.'

'If I thought he did, then I would have dismissed him by now. Why not show me what he's learnt?'

She looked disconcerted. 'You have to leave soon. I don't think . . .'

He laughed softly. 'I want to see the two of you together. Fetch him upstairs. I shall be waiting for you both in the playroom. That is where you train him, I believe?'

The blonde nodded and then, as Carlos left the room, she licked at her suddenly dry lips before ringing the bell to summon Felipe.

He answered promptly, and stood just inside the doorway smiling politely at her. He was the only member of staff that Carlos had brought with them from Rio, a muscular young man of medium height with straight jet-black hair and eyes as dark as coal.

Livia enjoyed teaching him to please her – it made a change from the relationship between her and Carlos – but she'd never envisaged having Carlos watch them together. Whenever he'd watched her with other men in the past, it had been men he'd chosen, friends or business colleagues. Also, they'd all been in control, just as Carlos always was. It was different with Felipe.

'I want you upstairs, in the playroom,' she said abruptly.

Felipe glanced nervously over his shoulder. 'But Senhor Rocca is still at home.'

She knew that somehow she had to convince him that Carlos wouldn't know. If he thought for one moment that his employer would be watching, he would never agree. He was besotted with Livia, but afraid of Carlos. 'He's just leaving,' she lied. 'Hurry, we won't have very long.'

Still Felipe hesitated, and Livia knew that she had to be firm with him. 'If I say I want you in the playroom now, then that's the end of it,' she said sharply. 'Come on, I'll lead the way if you're nervous.' She then walked out of the room and up the stairs, and to her relief she heard Felipe following behind her.

Pushing open the door to the room that Carlos called the playroom, she stood to one side to allow Felipe to pass. Then, the moment he'd stepped inside, she slammed the door shut behind him, turning the key in the lock before throwing it to Carlos, who was sitting at the foot of the bed.

Felipe gave a moan of horror. 'You said that Senhor Rocca was going out!'

Carlos studied the young Brazilian lad with interest. 'So, you were willing to sleep with my woman if I was out?'

'It's what she likes. She . . . she teaches me many things, some of them bad,' stammered Felipe.

'And do you enjoy these bad things?'

Felipe shook his head. 'No, not at all. I have a girlfriend back home. I am betraying her all the time.'

Carlos smiled. 'I shall be interested to see exactly how much you don't enjoy yourself,' he commented. 'As for betrayal, I don't for one moment believe you've thought about anyone but yourself during your time with Livia. It doesn't matter. I'm not angry, simply interested. Livia, please continue. Pretend I'm not here,' he added helpfully as Felipe made a sound of protest.

'Take off your clothes, Felipe,' said Livia. 'I want to see you naked.' After a nervous glance at his employer, Felipe obeyed, his fingers fumbling with his shirt buttons.

'Very nice,' murmured Livia appreciatively as he stood in front of her, his dark, muscular body rigid with tension. 'I'm pleased to see that the presence of Carlos has helped you control yourself for once. Now, I'm going to strip for you, but you're not allowed to get an erection yet. I don't really know why I'm telling you all this; you know the rules by now I'm sure.'

Slowly, sensuously, she began to remove her clothes. First she unfastened her skirt and let it fall to the floor, then she unbuttoned her blouse and peeled that off, before bending forward and unfastening her lacy bra, so that her heavy breasts fell free.

Finally she unfastened her stockings, removed them and then stepped out of her high-cut lace briefs. When all her clothing was lying in a heap on the floor, she moved closer to Felipe, until she was standing just in front of him. She didn't touch him, and didn't allow their bodies to touch, but instead ran her hands over her breasts and hips, sighing gently at each caress.

When she looked down, Felipe's penis was hardening, slowly rising upwards, and immediately she slapped it hard. He flinched, but her action only increased his excitement and still his thick cock continued to swell.

'I told you not to get an erection!' she snapped. 'Why are you so difficult to train? Now I'm going to have to punish you.'

Out of the corner of her eye, Livia saw Carlos move over to the window, presumably in case she needed to use the bed. Felipe saw him move as well, and she didn't know whether the look in his eyes was fear of her punishment or of Carlos watching his humiliation.

Taking some cord from a drawer, Livia fastened Felipe's hands behind his back, and then pushed him over to the padded stool in front of the dressing table. 'Bend over that,' she said, pushing on the nape of his neck. As soon as he'd obeyed her, she removed the leather belt from his discarded trousers and drew it through the fingers of her left hand. 'This will do nicely,' she remarked, and Felipe gave a muffled groan.

'Keep looking down at the floor,' she added, and then waited for what must have seemed to Felipe like endless seconds before striking him firmly across his buttocks with her first blow.

Felipe yelped with pain, and again Livia waited several seconds before striking him once more, just below where the first blow had fallen. As she continued to use the belt on him, Felipe's skin reddened but he was wriggling against the stool in a frenzy of ecstasy.

'Keep still!' she said angrily. 'If you come, I promise you you'll regret it.' At her words the Brazilian boy froze, and across the room Carlos nodded in appreciation. After a few more blows with the belt, Livia pulled Felipe upright by his tethered hands and then pushed him on to his back on the bed.

His erection was huge now, the tip purple and engorged.

'Naughty!' remarked Livia. 'It seems that you need further punishment. Your lack of self-control is disappointing, Felipe, particularly as Senhor Rocca is watching you. He'll think I'm a very poor teacher.'

Felipe stared silently at her, his eyes imploring her not to humiliate him further, but Livia was now so excited that nothing could have stopped her. In any case, it was evident that Felipe's body was enjoying itself, even if it was against his will.

'I know!' she exclaimed, with a laugh of delight. 'I'll pleasure us both at the same time. You know what I mean, I'm sure, Felipe. I remember your response to this particular form of punishment was most impressive when I last used it.'

'No, senhorita, please! I beseech you, not again.'

'You're so sweet when you beg,' replied Livia, rummaging in a box on the bedside table. 'Ah yes, here it is,' and she took out a long, thick, double-ended dildo.

As Felipe whimpered helplessly, she lubricated both ends with a clear gel and then ordered her victim to turn over on to his front.

Felipe knew better than to disobey Livia now. He knelt upright, and then lowered his upper body until his forehead was resting on the duvet. His hands were still fastened in front of him, and all he could do was wait.

Livia began to ease one end of the dildo between his tight buttocks, spreading the cheeks apart and rotating it as she pushed it in. Unluckily for Felipe, he couldn't stop himself from uttering a cry of pain, and this made her lose patience. She pushed it harder, and as soon as it was inside him, climbed on to the bed herself.

Her breathing was quick and shallow as she positioned herself over the servant lad's lower body, and when she impaled herself on the other end of the dildo she shuddered

41

with delight. Her shudder made the dildo vibrate, causing Felipe to moan again, but Livia ignored him.

She was caught up in the delirious excitement of having a man at her mercy. Every time she punished Felipe, she was suffused with a deep, throbbing ache that was only satisfied when she finally climaxed, preferably in a way that caused him pain as well as pleasure. It was a complete reversal of the way things were between her and Carlos, and the contrast between the two men made it all the more exciting.

Lost in the pursuit of her own pleasure, she thrust against the dildo with such force that it moved deeper inside Felipe. He gave a sharp cry, and then his hips started to move with frantic speed as his own climax approached.

'Wait!' gasped Livia, as she felt her internal muscles starting to tighten, but she could tell that Felipe was out of her control now. The sensations were too much for him, and nothing she did could halt his body's ascent to release.

It was then that Carlos made his move. Crossing to the bed, he reached beneath his servant's sweat-streaked body and gripped the young man's pulsating cock with his right hand, squeezing his thumb on the delicate underside while at the same time pressing hard on the opposite side with his forefinger.

Livia guessed what Carlos was doing, and the thought of Felipe's frustration and discomfort increased her own arousal. She bucked hard against the dildo, grabbing Felipe around the hips as she pushed herself closer to him.

He was sobbing with disappointment, unable to ejaculate because of Carlos's grip, and she'd never felt so powerful and commanding before. Her body's response was instantaneous. Within seconds of Felipe's first sob, she seemed to explode in a series of wrenching spasms of hot, liquid pleasure that left her exhausted and spent when they finally began to fade.

As she slid on to the bed, Carlos released their victim, but Felipe was no longer being stimulated and he remained kneeling face down on the bed, moaning quietly to himself.

Eventually Livia took pity on him. She untied his hands, then rolled him on to his back and lowered herself on to his erection. 'Come quickly,' she ordered him. 'But make sure I come again too.'

Felipe pushed his hips upwards and she felt him deep inside her, re-arousing her with the urgency of his movements. 'Yes!' she shouted in triumph, and seconds later they climaxed together. Flopping down on top of Felipe, she felt his tongue licking her nipples. This was something he always did after he'd climaxed, and she enjoyed it, but Carlos clearly didn't.

'That's enough!' he snapped. 'Training is over for today. You can go.'

Lazily, Livia rolled away and Felipe clambered off the bed, collected his clothes and hurried out of the room.

'So, you too enjoy controlling a person's pleasure,' remarked Carlos.

Livia wasn't certain if he was pleased or not. 'Only as a change,' she explained.

'Of course. In that case, you should enjoy helping me with Chloe's training.'

'I think I might,' she admitted.

Carlos ran his hands over her body, still damp from her lovemaking with Felipe. He massaged her breasts, stroked the sides of her belly and then began to tease the skin of her inner thighs until she felt herself starting to respond. With a contented sigh she closed her eyes, and immediately he removed his hands.

'Tomorrow, I want you to spend the night with friends,'

he told her as her eyes opened in surprise. 'I don't think Chloe will relax if you're here the first time.'

'Why did you stop touching me?' she asked plaintively.

'Perhaps I didn't enjoy watching you and Felipe,' he said casually. 'Remember now, tomorrow night I want the house to myself. You understand?'

'Of course,' she agreed, but after he'd left she didn't know how she felt about Chloe joining their household, or if she'd been wise to let him see her and Felipe together. With a man like Carlos Rocca, it was always hard to tell.

CHAPTER

7

Chloe felt uncomfortable as she got back to the London house where she was now living, and as she put her key in the front door she wondered how long it would be before she got used to it. Admittedly this was only her third night in her new room, so perhaps it wasn't surprising that she still felt like an intruder, but there was something about the atmosphere there that was putting her on edge.

'You're late,' called Carlos, coming out of the drawing room. 'You work too hard.'

'We're busy arranging next month's charity dinner. It's taking a lot of organising.'

'Remember to get me two tickets.'

'I don't think you'd enjoy it,' remarked Chloe, glancing around her. 'It's a little downmarket for you and Livia. The Covent Garden function will suit you more.'

'I'd still like tickets.'

'Lizzie will be pleased. She told me today that you'd offered to become our patron when Lady Somerville retires next month. She was very excited about it.'

'I hope she realises that it's because of you,' he said with a smile.

Chloe felt embarrassed. 'That's not true. You gave money

to the Brazilian branch of the charity long before you met me.'

'I never went to any of their social functions.'

'Well, I don't want you doing things just because of me,' said Chloe. 'You've done quite enough already, by letting me live here and—'

'That wasn't for your benefit, Chloe,' he said softly. 'It was for mine.'

She felt her stomach lurch, and started to walk towards the kitchen to get away from him, but he put out an arm and caught hold of her left wrist. 'Wait, don't go. We need to talk.'

Her chest was getting tight, making it difficult for her to breathe, and she could feel herself trembling. She wished that he'd let go of her; his fingers seemed to be burning into her flesh. 'What about?'

'I think you already know the answer to that.' His fingers tightened their grip.

'Let me go!' cried Chloe, twisting in his grasp.

Immediately he released her. 'It's all right, I didn't mean to scare you, but you must know how I feel about you. I want you, Chloe, I've wanted you from the first moment I saw you.'

She had known – deep down she'd been very aware of his desire – but it frightened her because she couldn't make sense of it. 'I'm not your type,' she protested as he took a step towards her. 'I don't know anything about people like you. I come from a different world, it's—'

'You mean you're not attracted to me?'

'That's not what I said, but it wouldn't work. You're used to women like Livia, sophisticated, experienced women. I've never slept with a man,' she added miserably.

His eyes were bright. 'That doesn't matter. It only makes you more special.' As he spoke, he started to run his hand up and down her bare right arm and the hypnotic movements soothed but also aroused her.

The skin beneath his fingers felt as though it was on fire, and when he lowered his head and kissed her gently on the mouth, she trembled violently as desire coursed through her. Instinctively, she put her arms round his neck, and immediately his kiss hardened and deepened.

He was murmuring in Portuguese, and although she had no idea what he was saying, the sound of his voice excited her. Then, as he picked her up and began to carry her up the stairs, she remembered his mistress. 'Where's Livia?' she gasped, freeing her mouth for a moment.

'Away for the night. Don't worry, relax. Leave everything to me.'

She was incapable of doing anything else. He took her into his bedroom, put her on the bed and then lay down beside her, making soothing sounds as he started to remove her clothes.

It was only when she felt his hands tugging at her panties that she began to feel frightened. 'No, wait!' she said hesitantly. 'I don't want . . . I'm not sure . . .'

'I just want to look at you,' he promised her, and then she was naked, and watched his eyes travelling over her. 'I'll make this good for you,' he promised her, as his hands began to move over her body.

Every feather-like touch, every soft, stroking movement made her flesh leap in response. She was almost overwhelmed by the intensity of the feelings he was arousing in her, and after a time she felt a strange ache between her thighs and started to move restlessly on the bed.

'Good, that's very good,' he said encouragingly. Then he quickly removed his own clothes before pulling her close to him so that her breasts were pressing against his chest. He kissed her hard for several minutes, before moving her on to her back and slipping a pillow beneath her hips.

When he moved over her, supporting himself on his forearms as he looked down at her, Chloe again felt a moment's fear. 'It's all right,' he assured her, and when she shivered, he moved down her body until his head was between her thighs.

'I want you to relax,' he said quietly, his hands spreading her legs further apart. His fingers moved gently, opening her up, and she moaned in shamed pleasure, then jumped as his tongue touched her delicate tissue with the lightest of movements.

Coloured lights flashed behind her closed eyelids as his tongue continued to excite her, and now she was moaning with desperate need. Her body felt swollen and tight, and her breasts were aching.

When he lifted his head she uttered a cry of disappointment, but then he was sliding up her again, and now she could feel his erection pressing against the opening where his tongue had been only moments before. For a second she stiffened against the invasion, but he fastened his mouth around her throbbing right nipple and her hips pushed upwards in response, enabling him to ease himself inside her.

Chloe felt a tingling begin between her thighs, and then a liquid heat started to spread through her lower belly. Carlos began to move his hips in a steady rhythm, increasing the pace gradually as Chloe's hips ground hard against his. She could hear herself uttering tiny cries of excitement as the tingling grew stronger and her entire body grew tense.

The sensations were wonderful, but she knew that they were leading her on to something even better, a pinnacle that was proving elusive as she struggled to reach it.

'Relax,' whispered Carlos. 'It will happen. Don't try too hard.'

She didn't know what he meant, all that she knew was that her body was clamouring for relief from the terrible tension building up inside her. She began to gasp as the heat spread through her, threatening to overwhelm her.

'No,' she cried. 'It's too much, I don't—'

Before she had time to finish speaking, Carlos pulled his head back, drawing her nipple out until it started to hurt, and then he closed his teeth around it and nipped at the rigid, delicate peak.

For a brief second, red-hot pain lanced through Chloe's breast. Startled, she began to cry out in protest, but almost immediately she felt her whole body draw in on itself, as though the centre of her was being pulled tightly upwards. Then her body was shaken by a series of violent muscular spasms and at last she was swamped with wave after wave of flooding pleasure.

Once she'd climaxed, Carlos put his hands under her hips and lifted her higher off the bed, plunging deeper inside her, lost in his own pursuit of satisfaction. She watched his face, saw the dark intensity of his desire, and when he came his head went back as he let out a tiny sigh of release.

A few minutes later he was lying beside her, stroking her hip with one hand as he pushed her dark curly hair back off her face with the other. 'Welcome to my kind of discipline,' he said quietly.

Chloe wanted to laugh. She'd never felt so light, so relaxed. 'If that's your idea of discipline, you must have misunderstood the meaning of the word!'

'You'll understand in time, I promise you.'

Reluctantly, Chloe started to come to her senses. 'What about Livia?' she murmured.

'Leave Livia to me. She's not your problem. Now sleep. Remember, this is only the beginning.'

She had no idea what he meant, but she was so tired she didn't really care. It was enough to know that they would have other times together.

For the next three weeks, Carlos visited Chloe in her room every other night. As she learned to relax more, the pleasure that he gave her intensified, and soon she found that on the nights when she was alone her body was longing for the sensations he aroused in her.

She started to think about sex all the time, even when she was at work. She'd drift off into daydreams, remembering the way his mouth and fingers had touched her writhing body, and she often failed to hear what people were saying to her.

'Have you fallen in love, Chloe?' asked Lizzie one day, when she'd had to repeat herself twice.

'Hardly. I don't know anyone in London!'

'Well, you're behaving like a girl who's in love. I thought perhaps this Senhor Rocca had introduced you to some young friend of his.'

'I hardly see him,' said Chloe, ashamed of the lie but more ashamed of the truth. 'He and Livia lead busy social lives.'

'As long as they include our events in their social lives, that's fine by me. You certainly must have made an impression on him. Not only did he offer you somewhere to stay, he's also upped his monthly donation in the past week. Make sure you stay on the right side of him, Chloe!'

'I'll try.'

'What's he like?' asked Lizzie curiously.

'In what way?'

'How old is he? And is he handsome in the way most Latin men are – all dark and brooding with wonderful liquid eyes?'

'He's an ordinary person, not the hero from the pages of some romantic novel!' replied Chloe, forcing herself to laugh.

'I know, but he's rich and influential, which normally makes any man attractive!'

'I don't know if you'd think him handsome or not,' muttered Chloe, wanting to change the subject because all she could think about was the way his blue eyes would watch her intently as she climaxed, as though he was assessing her in some way.

'It's a pity you're so naïve about men. Still, perhaps that's what he likes about you. Men of the world admire innocence and purity, probably because they don't see much of it.'

Chloe wondered if that was true, and was the reason why Carlos seemed so fascinated by her. She hoped not, because if it was, then he was doing his best to change her. She was no longer the innocent she'd been when he'd met her, in which case he might soon tire of her. The prospect of losing their nights of passion was terrible, and for the rest of the day she worried that Lizzie was right.

That night he was due to visit her again, and as she lay waiting for him she could feel her body trembling slightly with excited anticipation. At midnight, the time he usually came, she heard her door opening and switched on her bedside lamp.

'You look worried,' he remarked, taking off his clothes and pulling the covers off her before lying down at her side.

'I'm not worried.'

He stroked her face and hair. 'Are you sure?'

She didn't want him to know how much her body craved the pleasure he brought it, or how much she was afraid of losing him, so she kept quiet about her chat with Lizzie. 'Quite sure,' she said firmly.

'That's good. I like to know I've got your full attention.' With that he began to stroke each of her breasts in turn, lightly at first and then more firmly, until they were swollen and the nipples hard.

As Chloe gave a sigh of pleasure, he began to kiss her belly and then moved his head lower and started sucking on the delicate flesh of her inner thighs. Closing her eyes, she felt the tension start building behind her clitoris, and when his tongue moved lazily along the channel between her inner sex lips, she felt the first tingles of an impending orgasm.

This was her favourite moment, the few seconds when she was balanced between tension and release, and her breath caught in her throat. Then, with shocking abruptness, his tongue was removed and she was left teetering on the brink of her climax.

'Why did you stop?' she cried, opening her eyes and seeing him gazing down at her.

'Because tonight is when you start to learn about the discipline.'

There was a dull throbbing between her thighs, and she felt her hips jerk upwards as her body started to search for satisfaction. 'I don't know what you mean.'

He smiled at her. 'I know. That's what makes tonight so exciting.'

Chloe felt completely bewildered. Everything had been going so well. Her body was tight with tension, and she was damp between her thighs. Carlos had tutored her to enjoy satisfaction, but now he was cruelly withholding her pleasure.

As she tried to make sense of it, he got up and opened her bedroom door. Turning her head, she saw Livia come in, and immediately she sat up. 'No! I don't want her here. What's happening, Carlos?'

'Sshh!' he murmured, touching the side of her face with his right hand. 'You're someone who understands the meaning of discipline, who needed it to make sense of your life. Now I'm going to bring discipline into your pleasure. It will make the rewards all the greater, but you have to do as you're told.'

Chloe felt a mixture of fear and anger. 'What if I won't do as I'm told?'

'Then I'm afraid I'll have to punish you,' said Carlos regretfully.

Livia glanced at Chloe. 'She doesn't want to do it. Let her go,' she said contemptuously. 'I told you she wasn't our kind of person, Carlos. Go on, Chloe. Get away now, while you still can. No one's forcing you to stay.'

'Good,' said Chloe, and she started to get out of bed, but then she saw a glint of triumph in Livia's eyes and hesitated. Her skin was still tingling with excitement, her body throbbing with the passion Carlos had aroused in her. If she left now, she would probably never know such pleasure again. In any case, she was secretly intrigued by what she'd heard, and the fact that Livia so clearly wanted her to go was another incentive for her to stay.

'On second thoughts, I think I would like to learn more about your kind of discipline,' she said slowly, looking directly at Carlos as she spoke.

His lips parted a little, and he nodded his approval. 'That's good. However, if you choose to stay, then there can be no turning back. You're putting yourself into my hands, and I may not offer you the chance to leave again until I've taught you all that I want you to know.'

A frisson of fear ran through her, but she didn't hesitate. 'I understand,' she said quietly.

'Excellent. Now, lie back on the bed. Livia's tongue is just as skilled as mine. She'll take over where I left off, but I don't want you to climax with her. I want you to wait for me. Is that clear?'

'Quite clear,' said Chloe, lying on the bed again. She couldn't really believe that she was doing this, that she was going to have another woman's tongue touching her so intimately, but she wanted to please Carlos, wanted to prove to him that she was capable of doing anything he demanded of her.

While Livia stripped off her negligée and put her head between Chloe's thighs, Carlos settled himself on the edge of the bed, right beside Chloe, and looked at her tense, aroused body with interest.

'You'll find it difficult not to come, I imagine,' he said casually.

She didn't think that he was right. It was having *his* tongue on her that aroused her, knowing he was touching and caressing her. Livia's attentions wouldn't be the same.

'Remember, come and you'll be disciplined,' he reminded her, and then she saw him glance at Livia. 'Right, you can begin.'

As Livia's slim fingers opened Chloe up, she felt her body stiffen in resistance. It seemed wrong, but then as the other woman's tongue moved around the entrance to her aching vagina, she groaned with pleasure.

Livia was an expert, and when she began to flick her tongue from side to side over the swollen nub of the clitoris itself, Chloe felt her orgasm building fast. The first tingles grew rapidly into a hot, aching need and her belly was tight.

'Be careful,' murmured Carlos, and she struggled to subdue her wanton body, to stop the insidious waves of liquid heat from engulfing her.

'You like that, don't you?' murmured Livia, and then for a moment she removed her tongue and Chloe gasped with

relief. It was short-lived, because next Livia drew the tip of her tongue over the entrance to Chloe's urethra, making her jerk with shock as the sensations intensified. As her clitoris began to withdraw beneath its protective hood, Livia carefully held it back and waited for a few seconds before drawing the small collection of nerve-endings into her mouth and sucking lightly on it.

'Discipline yourself,' said Carlos sharply, as Chloe's body began to writhe helplessly on the bed, but she couldn't. It was hopeless, and she knew it. As Livia continued to lick and suck at the centre of her sexuality, the warm glow spread and her tense muscles abruptly spasmed as she spiralled into a wrenching orgasm.

Watching Chloe's slight body heaving helplessly, and hearing the despair behind her cries of ecstasy, Carlos felt himself harden with excitement. She'd been so certain that she would be able to obey him, so confident that Livia wouldn't bring her to orgasm, that watching her fail was twice as sweet as he'd expected.

'Your self-control leaves a lot to be desired,' he remarked dispassionately. 'Livia, fetch the stool over here. I shall carry out her punishment myself.'

Chloe stared up at him, her dark eyes fearful now that the final moments of pleasure were over. 'I tried,' she protested. 'It's your fault. You've taught my body to respond like that.'

'And now I intend to teach it how to be more disciplined. Don't make a fuss, Chloe. You chose to stay, and you knew what would happen if you failed.'

Her head drooped, and she didn't protest any more, even when he caught hold of her hands and pulled her off the bed.

'Keep your hands out in front of you,' he instructed her,

and watched her almond-shaped grey eyes widen in fear as he fastened her wrists together with a pair of padded handcuffs. She was clearly shocked, and when he pushed her facedown across the stool she began to struggle.

Livia, who was sliding a small pillow beneath Chloe's hips, laughed softly. 'What did you expect, a written warning?'

Chloe continued to struggle, but Carlos held her firmly in place until Livia was able to fasten a broad leather strap round the young girl's body, buckling it beneath the stool. The strap was tight, biting into Chloe's creamy flesh, and she whimpered.

'Keep quiet, or you'll be gagged as well,' said Carlos, and his words silenced her immediately. She'd become very still, probably, he thought, because any movement only made the strap round her waist dig into her delicate skin. He watched her for a moment.

Her head was down, her long, wavy dark hair tumbling round the sides of her face. Her manacled hands were brushing the carpet and there was a fine sheen of perspiration covering her shoulders and the nape of her neck. Carlos could smell her fear, and it acted like an aphrodisiac on him.

Livia moved quietly between Chloe's legs, kneeling down on the floor as she parted the other girl's thighs. Silently, without taking his eyes off the fastened girl, Carlos picked up a thin whip from the top of his dressing table and then returned to stand over the trembling, helpless Chloe.

Chloe couldn't believe what was happening to her. It was like a nightmare. She could never remember being so frightened, and yet the terrible thing was that she was aroused. She was damp between her thighs, and her nipples were tingling. It made no sense to her.

She was aware of Carlos moving round the room, and

could feel Livia's hands between her legs, but she didn't know what was going to happen next. All she could do was wait.

She heard the sound of the whip before she felt it. There was a sharp cracking noise, swiftly followed by a hot burning sensation across the top of her buttocks. Chloe had never been hit before, and she gave a cry of astonishment mingled with pain. No one said anything to her, and when she tried to turn her head to see what was happening, Carlos roughly forced her face down again.

The second blow was just underneath the first, and delivered with greater force. This time the initial burst of pain made her whole body jump, and immediately the wide strap bit into her flesh, adding to her discomfort. She couldn't stop herself from whimpering, and when a third blow caught the top of the backs of her thighs she felt tears welling up in her eyes.

'Relax,' murmured Carlos, running a hand down the length of her spine as her body spasmed with shock. 'Soon the pleasure will come.'

This time the whip fell higher up, the tip catching the side of her left breast, and she screamed as the burning pain coursed through her upper body. Then, just as she felt sure that she couldn't bear it any longer, the burning feeling changed and became a kind of perverse pleasure.

Every time her body jerked with the pain of the whip, the strap round her middle pressed her down more tightly against the cushion beneath her, which stimulated her even more. When she felt Livia's knowing fingers sliding up and down the moist channel between her labia, Chloe moaned with pleasure.

The sweet ache that she'd grown to love was building rapidly, low in her belly, and she could feel her nipples hardening. Her muscles tightened, and coloured lights started to flash behind her closed eyelids as Livia lightly brushed against the side of her clitoris.

Now all the pain, discomfort and humiliation was forgotten as her climax approached. Her head went back, and it was then that Carlos spoke.

'Not yet, Chloe. This was to punish you for failing to delay your orgasm. Don't make me have to punish you twice in one night for the same offence.'

Chloe could hear herself gasping as Livia continued to stimulate her, and the climax drew inexorably nearer. She didn't want to come, didn't want to be punished again, but her body had a mind of its own. Desperately she attempted to shut out the delicate movements of Livia's fingers, and she slowed her frantic breathing to try and relax the tight muscles that were bunched ready for the delicious moment of release.

Gradually she felt herself taking control, felt the darting tingles begin to ebb away as she concentrated hard on the self-discipline that Carlos was trying to teach her. Despite Livia redoubling her efforts, the moment of crisis passed and Chloe's head fell forward again.

'Excellent!' exclaimed Carlos. 'You're clearly going to be a good pupil. That's enough, Livia, you can stop now.' A wave of relief swept over Chloe, because Livia was clever and had begun tapping the side of Chloe's clitoris with the soft pad of her index finger, an exquisite sensation.

Carlos unbuckled the belt holding Chloe to the stool and pulled her upright. She stood in front of him, naked, still handcuffed, and swaying a little from the effort of subduing her body's natural responses.

His lips parted and then the almost detached expression on his face changed abruptly as his eyes grew bright. 'That's how I wanted to see you,' he muttered thickly. 'That's how the discipline works.'

As he spoke, he grabbed her round the waist and threw her roughly on to the bed, pushing her fastened hands above her head and pinning them down with his right hand, while his left pinched her right nipple hard.

She didn't dare make a sound in case he stopped. Her skin was burning, and she ached so badly between her thighs that when he thrust into her she wanted to cry out with gratitude because at last he was satisfying the dreadful need that was beginning to consume her.

He'd never taken her so abruptly, without a single caress or kiss, but she wrapped her legs round his waist and tightened herself around him so that they both climaxed at the same moment, and she shuddered with the painful intensity of her orgasm.

Carlos was breathing heavily when he withdrew, and he glanced down at her with a look of surprise in his eyes.

'No wonder you gave up the idea of becoming a nun,' he remarked drily. 'Tomorrow, you and I must talk.'

Before Chloe could reply, he got off the bed and left the bedroom, taking Livia with him.

CHAPTER

8

The next morning Chloe got up early, determined to be out of the house before Carlos had a chance to speak to her. She didn't want to talk to him, couldn't face any discussion about what had gone on the night before. All she wanted was to get away from the house, and then try to come to terms with what she'd allowed to happen to her.

Quickly she boiled the kettle and made herself a cup of coffee. It was still only eight o'clock, so she felt quite safe; eight-thirty was the earliest she'd ever seen Carlos up and about, and Mrs Clarke, the housekeeper, didn't start work until nine. However, when she heard the kitchen door open, she knew, even before she turned her head, that he'd decided to make today an exception, and her stomach fluttered.

'You're up early,' he commented. 'Will the office be open if you go in now?'

'I've got my own set of keys, because I'm often the last to leave.'

'What a diligent young lady you are. I hope your supervisor realises what a little treasure she has working for her.'

'Lizzie appreciates what I do, if that's what you mean.'

Carlos looked at her with interest, his eyes once more

seeming to assess her. She found this habit of his unsettling, but at the same time exciting. It was as though he wasn't seeing the persona she presented to the world, but some private part of her that she didn't yet know about herself.

'I want you back here by seven tonight,' he said after a pause. 'I hope that won't present any difficulties?'

'Actually it will. We're having a committee meeting to discuss the dinner. It won't be over by then.'

'In that case you'll have to leave early.'

'I can't do that,' replied Chloe firmly. 'What does it matter to you when I get back?'

'There's something that I want you to do tonight, and it's planned for seven o'clock. Punctuality is in itself a kind of discipline, as I'm sure the nuns taught you.'

'I don't think I want to bring the nuns into this discussion. Your kind of discipline has nothing to do with religion,' she said hotly.

'I never said it had. There are many kinds of discipline, and after last night it's clear to me that you can adjust to them all very well. Watching you was a revelation,' he added softly.

Immediately Chloe became aware of her right nipple, which was still sore from when he'd pinched it just before she'd climaxed. A blush of embarrassment stained her cheeks, and she had a job to stop herself from touching the tender breast.

'I've changed my mind about your form of discipline,' she said, hoping he couldn't hear the slight tremor in her voice. 'I don't think I do want to learn about it after all.'

Carlos stepped closer to her. Very slowly he put out his right hand, and then began to stroke her dark hair, pushing it back off her face. 'What's the matter? Are you afraid of learning the truth about yourself?'

'I don't belong in your world. I told you that when you asked me to stay here. I'm not sophisticated like Livia, I'm—'

'You're a sensualist, Chloe. Don't try and deny it, especially to yourself.'

'Why shouldn't I deny it, if I want to? Why is this so important to you?'

His blue eyes darkened. 'That's a good question. You fascinate me. I want to know more about you, the real you. Also, I want to set you free.'

Chloe shook her head. 'I think you want to imprison me.'

Catching hold of her shoulders, Carlos stared into Chloe's eyes. 'You're wrong. I can liberate you, but you have to trust me.'

'After what happened last night?'

With a smile he released her, and turning away started to make himself a cup of coffee. 'Are you trying to tell me that you didn't enjoy last night?'

'No, what I'm trying to tell you is that I don't want it to go any further.'

'What are you afraid of if it does?' he asked quietly. 'Think carefully before you reply.'

Chloe bit on her bottom lip. 'I'm afraid of myself,' she confessed.

'Don't be; let me release your true sexuality, and I'll help you come to terms with what you discover.'

'But why does learning about my sexuality have to involve rules, and discipline?'

'Because it heightens all the sensations, and multiplies all the pleasures. Delayed gratification is far sweeter than instant satisfaction.'

Chloe shivered. 'What happens when it's all over? When I've learnt all there is to know about myself?'

'Then we think of how you can best use your gifts. Don't

worry, I'll be here for you. So, will you be back at seven tonight?'

Chloe wished that she could just say no and walk away, but this morning Carlos was like a magician weaving a magic spell around her, and now she did want to be part of his strange world. 'Yes,' she murmured.

'Excellent. When you're discussing the charity dinner, tell your supervisor that I want to sit at the same table as you on the evening.'

'I can't do that!' exclaimed Chloe. 'You'll be at the top table. I should think I'll be at the one nearest the kitchen door.'

'If we're not at the same table, I won't attend. It's as simple as that.'

'I don't think they're expecting you anyway. Like I said, it's too low-key for you.'

'Arrange it, Chloe. I want to sit beside you for the evening. I promise that I shall make it worth the charity's while if they indulge my wish.'

'This may come as a surprise to you,' said Chloe slowly, 'but your money won't buy you everything you want in life.'

He laughed. 'Of course it won't, but it will buy me most things and it will most certainly buy you a place at the top table – especially as I'll be the patron by then!' Glancing at his watch, he raised an eyebrow at her. 'Won't you be late if you don't leave soon?'

Chloe looked at the kitchen clock. 'Oh no! I was early too.' Running out of the house, she heard Carlos calling out after her, reminding her to be back at the house by seven o'clock.

'You want a place at the top table?' asked Lizzie in astonishment.

All the committee, who were seated round the table, were staring at Chloe, and she wished the earth would open up and swallow her, but she had no choice. She had to do as Carlos had asked, if only for the donation to the cause that her success would bring.

'It's not that *I* want to sit at the top table. Carlos Rocca himself has requested it,' she muttered.

Lizzie looked thoughtfully at Chloe as the rest of the women whispered among themselves. 'I see,' she said slowly. 'Well, he's a very generous and important man, and I'm sure none of us had even expected him to come, so unless anyone objects, I'll seat you next to him if that's what he wants. No doubt you'll find an opportunity to pass the good news on to him,' she added.

'I'm really sorry,' apologised Chloe. 'I'd much rather be somewhere obscure, but . . .'

'We get the picture,' said one of the older committee members, and the look she gave Chloe was far from friendly. 'You don't have to work day *and* night for the charity, dear.'

Lizzie gave Chloe a quick smile. 'Don't take it to heart,' she whispered, reaching out and giving the younger girl's hand a squeeze. 'They're all jealous.'

Glancing down, Chloe caught sight of Lizzie's watch, and saw that it was nearly six-thirty. 'I've got to go,' she gasped. 'Sorry, I have to be somewhere by seven.'

'But we haven't finished,' said Lizzie.

'Tell me about it tomorrow,' Chloe called over her shoulder, and then she was running out of the building and off down the street.

It was one minute to seven when she closed the front door behind her, and she leant against it for a moment, trying to catch her breath and waiting for her heart to stop racing.

'You were nearly late,' said Carlos, coming out of his study.

'I was on time.'

'Yes; I'm almost sorry. I was quite looking forward to devising a punishment for you.' He smiled as he spoke, but only with his mouth; his eyes showed his true feelings, and Chloe offered up a silent prayer of thanks to Lizzie and her watch.

'You can eat later,' continued Carlos. 'Come upstairs. I've got someone waiting for you.'

Slowly Chloe followed him up the wide staircase, and there was a fluttering feeling in the pit of her stomach that was a mixture of nerves and excitement. He led her along the landing and into a small room at the far end of the passage, a room that she'd never noticed before.

The curtains were drawn and the room was dark except for a small spotlight set high in the wall directly opposite the door. She'd half expected to find Livia waiting for her, or even Livia and another girl, but nothing had prepared her for what she saw.

Standing erect in the spotlight, his tanned, muscular body gleaming with oil, was a young man. His hands were fastened behind his back, and around his impressive erection there were three metal rings.

'This is Felipe,' said Carlos. 'Livia has been getting him ready for the past hour, but from now on he's all yours. Say hello to Chloe, Felipe.'

'Good evening, Chloe,' said Felipe, smiling at her as though their meeting was the most natural thing in the world.

She glanced at Carlos, not knowing what she was expected to say or do. He smiled back at her, but it was a different kind of smile. 'He's all yours. Enjoy yourself for as long as you like. Livia has trained him well. He won't come

65

until you've finished entertaining us. I think it would be nice if he gave you four orgasms, don't you?'

'What's he going to do?' asked Chloe nervously.

'That's entirely up to you. He's your slave, you instruct him.' He turned away to speak to Livia, who was standing by the wall. 'Livia, sit here with me and let Chloe take over now. You can have him at the end, when Chloe's finished.'

'But I can't . . . I don't know . . .'

Carlos began to look impatient. 'This isn't difficult, Chloe. Use him to pleasure yourself. Everything you need is in the room here. Please get started. We don't want Felipe to lose his enthusiasm for the task.'

'Does he have to stay tied?'

'Yes. If you need him unbound for anything in particular, then you must re-fasten his hands afterwards. Hurry now.'

Realising that Felipe couldn't help her undress, Chloe began to unbutton her blouse, but then Carlos took over, almost tearing the buttons off in his haste. Within seconds she was naked, and she saw Felipe's erection harden as he looked at her body.

Seeing this, Chloe felt a rush of power. The handsome young man clearly desired her, but she would be in control, able to choose exactly how he pleasured her. Forgetting the two watchers in the far corner of the room, she walked over to Felipe.

'Kneel down,' she said softly, and immediately he fell to his knees, looking up at her anxiously. She could feel her juices starting to flow, and stood over him with her legs parted. 'I want you to use your tongue on me,' she murmured.

'You give him orders, not requests,' said Carlos. 'You have authority, use it.'

'Use your tongue on me.' This time her voice was stronger, harsher, and it had the desired effect. Felipe moved his head between her parted thighs, and as she opened herself with her hands his tongue swept upwards, searching for the tight bud that was already throbbing sweetly.

When he found it, his tongue stroked the shaft of her clitoris with slow, expert movements that quickly had her moaning with excitement. Then, as she ground herself against the delicious pressure, he flicked the tip of his tongue into her vagina and pressed it upwards. Immediately a deep, throbbing pleasure shot through her and her legs began to tremble.

She was on the verge of coming now, could feel the tiny pinprick of pleasure building steadily, and when he twirled the tip of his tongue on the top of the throbbing clitoris itself her body spasmed and she whimpered with gratitude.

'That's one,' said Livia. 'Enjoying yourself, Felipe?'

Chloe stepped away from the kneeling Felipe and glanced down at him. His penis was painfully hard, and the three metal rings meant that it was impossible for his erection to subside. On a sudden impulse, she reached down and squeezed him gently, just beneath the velvet-soft tip. With a gasp, Felipe edged backwards, his face contorted in pain.

'Don't move unless you're ordered to,' said Carlos sternly. 'Chloe, he knows better than that. Here, you must punish him,' and he handed her a latex whip. Not daring to disobey, she took it from him, and then, raising her arm, brought it down across Felipe's bent back.

She struck him twice before telling him to get to his feet, and to her surprise, when she looked at him again, he was even more aroused than before. At the back of the room Livia gave a soft laugh, rejoicing in Felipe's burgeoning excitement.

Now Chloe's body wanted satisfaction again, and she unfastened Felipe's hands before lying down on the pile of cushions in the middle of the room. 'Just use your hands on me,' she ordered him. Her body tingled with anticipation as he obediently positioned himself to her left and began to caress her breasts, lightly at first but then more firmly.

When Chloe let out a soft sigh, he moved one hand between her legs, easing them apart before dipping a finger deep inside her and spreading her juices between her inner sex lips.

Chloe wriggled as a warm glow began to flicker behind her clitoris. She could see Felipe watching her face closely, his soft dark eyes studying her face for every reaction. As he ran a finger up and down the right side of her clitoris she could feel his erection nudging against her hip bone, and heard his breath snag in his throat.

'You make me want to come,' he whispered, putting his mouth close to her ear.

She knew that she did, and this increased her excitement. Frantically she pushed her hips upwards, searching for that moment of release. Felipe's fingertip had been working in the same rhythm for some time now, and the pressure was building deep in her belly, but no matter how much she tried she couldn't quite climax.

Deftly, Felipe moved his finger to the top of her aching bud and then brushed it from side to side across the tip. It felt as though a surge of electricity was shooting through her, and a harsh, piercing pleasure seared her body as she thrashed around on the cushions with delight.

'Two orgasms,' said Carlos quietly. 'Quickly, Felipe, turn her over and stimulate her other entrance.'

'No!' cried Chloe. 'That's not what I want.'

Felipe hesitated, but when Carlos started to rise from his

chair he did as he'd been told and flipped Chloe over, so that she was facing the other way. Reaching round her, he slipped a finger into her mouth and instinctively she sucked on it, drawing it in deeper, pretending it was his ringed cock plunging into her, satisfying her aching vagina.

Felipe let his finger stay there for a few seconds, then withdrew it and eased it between her buttocks, which were resting against his naked, tightly muscled belly. She felt the moistened finger moving in slow circles around the outside of her rectum, slowly arousing small darts of excitement. As she began to relax, enjoying the sensation, he abruptly inserted his finger inside her and her body stiffened as she tried to draw away.

It was only then, when he knelt over her and held her still, that she realised Carlos had remained close to the cushions, meaning that she was now in bondage to him. Even as she struggled, Felipe was stroking the inside of her rectum, teasing the incredibly sensitive walls with the lightest of touches.

It felt as though all her internal muscles were being drawn inwards, and despite the slight discomfort, she knew that yet another orgasm was building inexorably within her. She was ashamed of her body's reaction, but was again frantic for release, and pressed herself backwards so that his finger penetrated her more deeply.

The discomfort immediately increased, and she gave a cry of protest, but Carlos ignored her and continued to keep her shoulders pinned to the cushions. Felipe moved his left hand round beneath Chloe's body and between her thighs. Within seconds he began to caress the sides of her clitoris as well, and after a few seconds of this combined stimulation an orgasm swept through her as her body jackknifed with the cruel intensity of the sensation.

'Your third orgasm,' said Carlos, satisfaction evident in his voice.

Felipe stopped stimulating Chloe and lay motionless behind her, waiting to see what he had to do next.

Determined to regain control, Chloe sat up and looked at Carlos. 'I want Felipe's hands tied behind him again.'

'Then do it yourself.'

Her fingers fumbled with the leather cuffs, and she had to order him off the bed, but finally she had him as he'd been when she'd entered the room, hands bound behind his back, naked and helpless, standing waiting for her to do what she liked with him.

For the first time she was able to appreciate the pleasure of it all, and her overstimulated body drove her on as she walked towards Felipe. She pushed at his shoulders until he was standing against the wall, then wrapped her arms round his neck and pulled herself up his oiled body.

Felipe braced himself as well as he could with his hands tied, and when she wrapped her legs round his waist she saw a look of fear in his eyes, but she didn't care. All that she wanted was to have him inside her, to feel his rigid erection sliding into her, with the metal rings touching her internal walls.

He was bigger than she'd expected, and she caught her breath for a moment as she impaled herself on him, but then some deep primeval instinct took over and she moved herself frantically up and down on him. The cold touch of the metal rings against her hot, damp flesh was exquisite, and she moved faster and faster as the first gentle tingles expanded and spread.

Felipe was moaning now, clearly terrified of climaxing himself, but Chloe didn't care what happened to him. The heat was rushing through her belly, her throbbing breasts were being caressed by his chest as she moved, and finally, with one massive explosion, she came and the contractions seemed to go on for ever.

When the last flickers of pleasure had completely died away, she lifted herself off him and slid down to the floor. Only when she felt the thick stickiness between her thighs did she realise that she'd made Felipe come as well.

'You did well,' said Carlos, helping her up and putting an arm round her shoulders. 'I have to confess that I hadn't expected you to show such aptitude for domination.'

Chloe was surprised as well, surprised and ashamed. 'It doesn't seem right,' she murmured.

'You enjoyed it, didn't you?'

'Yes, but . . .'

'Now you begin to learn the advantages of the discipline. Without me to guide you, how would you ever have learnt this about yourself?'

'But what about Felipe?' she asked, as she saw Livia leading the still bound young man out of the room, riding crop in hand.

'I thought that Felipe looked to be enjoying himself too. People get sexual pleasure in many strange ways, Chloe, as you're beginning to learn.'

At that moment, Felipe's voice could be heard crying out in obvious pain, and Chloe took a step towards the door through which he and Livia had gone. Carlos tightened his grip on her. 'Leave them alone. It's Livia's turn to enjoy herself now, and Felipe did fail. He's well trained, and knew what to expect once he lost control of himself.'

Chloe liked having his arm round her, and her body was still glowing with satisfaction, but she couldn't quite shake off her feelings of guilt.

'I need to shower,' she said abruptly.

Later that night, when she was trying to get to sleep, she

71

found herself playing the scene with Felipe over and over in her mind. It still had the power to arouse her, and it was only by masturbating herself to orgasm that she was finally able to sleep.

CHAPTER

9

In the morning, Chloe lay in bed thinking about everything that had happened to her since she'd moved into Carlos's house. Now, in the cold light of day, the events of the night before made her feel ashamed. She couldn't believe what she'd done, and how much she'd enjoyed it. It was as though Carlos had her in some kind of spell, but it was a spell that she knew she had to break.

At eight o'clock, before anyone was up, she packed a few essential things into an overnight bag and slipped out of the house. Unknown to her, Carlos was watching as she walked down the front path, her bag over her shoulder.

It was too early to go into the office, so she decided to stop off at a nearby café. There she sat at a table by the window drinking coffee, looking out at the people hurrying by on their way to work. For the first time, she wondered about other people's secret lives, and whether there were many like Carlos and Livia.

When she finally got up to leave, a young man from a nearby table also stood up and held the door open to let her through. She smiled her thanks, and he smiled back. Idly, her mind registered the fact that he was very attractive in a fresh-faced way, something she wouldn't have thought about before she'd become involved with Carlos.

Walking swiftly away, she was overtaken by the young man, who then turned and started to move towards her. Chloe's first thought was that she'd left her purse on the table, and he'd picked it up for her.

'I hope you don't mind me chasing after you,' he said apologetically. 'It's just that I was watching you back at the café, and you looked a little lost. I wondered if you were new to London?'

'No, I'm not,' said Chloe briskly.

'That's a pity. I was going to offer to show you around one evening.'

'Thank you, but that's not necessary. If you'll excuse me, I'm going to be late for work if I don't hurry.'

He looked disappointed. 'Perhaps we could go out for a meal one evening then?'

Chloe couldn't believe her ears. She was wearing a plain summer dress and hadn't even put on any make-up that morning. There didn't seem to be any reason why a handsome young man would want to pick her up, let alone think she'd be interested.

'No, thank you,' she said firmly, afraid that she was subconsciously sending out the wrong kind of signals after her encounter with Felipe the night before.

'We'd have a good time,' said the stranger confidently.

Looking directly into his face, Chloe, with her new-found experience, knew that he was right. She felt a fluttering in her stomach and a desire to know what it would be like with this man. Slowly an idea formed in her mind.

'I can't make dinner,' she said slowly. 'I'm working late. I'm connected with a charity that helps Brazilian street children. Why don't you call in at our office instead and make a donation that will enable them to be fed?'

The stranger's eyes sparkled. 'If I do, will you at least come out for a drink with me tonight?'

'Yes, a drink would be nice,' she agreed. Then, before she had time to change her mind, she gave him one of the charity's cards and hurried off, wondering if she'd gone completely mad.

'What's with the suitcase?' asked Lizzie as Chloe sat down at her workstation. 'Hope you're not leaving Senhor Rocca's mansion. We don't want to upset our next patron before he's taken over.'

'I hope I'm not expected to run my private life the way Carlos wants me to, just to keep the money rolling in,' retorted Chloe.

'Hey, steady on! It was a joke. Is there some kind of problem?'

Chloe, who was thoroughly confused by her own behaviour minutes earlier, shook her head. 'Of course not. This is an overnight bag, that's all. I'm seeing a friend tonight.'

'Right,' said Lizzie, sounding totally unconvinced. 'I'll leave you to deal with the phone. The list for cold calling is pinned to the notice board. Start after the last ticked name. Victoria was doing some yesterday, but she spends more time on the phone to her friends than possible supporters. Unfortunately I can't get rid of her; her father's one of the founders.'

'It's strange: I left religious orders because the charity was corrupt, but it's no better here,' commented Chloe.

'That's a dreadful thing to say!' exclaimed Lizzie. 'We don't pay backhanders to people, or bribe anyone. We just have to be willing to be flexible about things, but that's true in every walk of life.'

'We'd do anything to keep our chief benefactors happy,'

replied Chloe, taking down the list and seeing that Victoria had only managed eight phone calls in an afternoon.

'You might,' said Lizzie frostily, 'but I certainly wouldn't. Perhaps that's why you're the one Carlos Rocca wants sitting next to him at the dinner next month. If you're annoyed with yourself, Chloe, please don't take it out on me.'

Chloe sighed. 'Sorry, Lizzie. Think I got out of bed the wrong side this morning. I'll feel better once I'm busy.'

Soon she was immersed in phone calls, and when she went out into the front office at midday, she'd almost convinced herself that her bizarre early-morning encounter had never happened. The sight of the blond-haired stranger handing over a cheque to a smiling Lizzie soon shattered that delusion.

'That's very generous of you,' said Lizzie, putting the cheque into a black metal box. 'How did you get to hear about us?'

'I met that young lady this morning,' he replied, looking straight at Chloe.

'Really? I must send her out canvassing for us on a daily basis then.'

The young man smiled. 'I'm sure she'd do very well. I'll collect you from here this evening if you like,' he added to Chloe. 'What time do you expect to finish?'

'About nine; we've got a committee meeting that starts at seven.'

'Nine it is then. See you later.'

Lizzie watched him go and then turned to Chloe. 'Is that the friend you said you were staying with tonight? If so, you seem to make friends very quickly.'

'Of course I'm not staying with him,' muttered Chloe. 'We're having a drink together, that's all.'

Lizzie put a hand on Chloe's arm. 'Be careful,' she said softly. 'This isn't like you, Chloe. You're changing, but I don't think you understand that behaving like this can be dangerous. You've had a very protected life and—'

'I'll be fine,' Chloe assured her, although she wasn't certain that was true. The one thing she did know was that she'd been over-hasty in thinking that she must leave her lodgings that morning. The truth was, it was already too late for her to leave Carlos. He'd started to awaken the dark side of her sexuality, and she needed him to teach her more before she could hope to be ready to go out into the world and cope with her new-found knowledge on her own.

She'd go back tonight, and he needn't ever know she'd intended to leave. First, though, she would have one drink with the blond stranger.

'Sorry I'm late. These committee meetings always go on longer than they're meant to,' said Chloe as she got into the dark-blue BMW that was parked on a double yellow line outside the building where she worked.

'I'm relieved you're here. I had a feeling you might stand me up at the last minute.'

'I nearly did,' she confessed, putting her overnight case on the back seat. 'You know, I don't think you ever told me your name.'

'Let's leave it that way,' he said softly. 'It makes it all the more exciting, don't you think?'

She nodded, aware that she was already trembling with excitement. 'Where are we going?'

'You'll see. Sit back and enjoy the ride.'

Chloe began to feel nervous. 'I want to know where we're going.'

The stranger turned his head to look at her, and smiled his pleasant smile. 'For a drink, of course. That's what you wanted, isn't it?'

'I meant, which pub are we going to?'

'It's in Richmond, near the river. You'll like it.'

'We haven't got time to go to Richmond,' she protested. 'It's nine o'clock already.' He didn't answer her. Instead he put a classical CD on the player and turned up the volume, drowning out any further attempts at conversation on her part.

As they sped through the streets of London, jumping lights and overtaking on bends, Chloe sat in terrified silence, remembering Lizzie's words of warning and wishing that she'd heeded them. It was too late now. All she could do was wait until the car stopped and then make a run for it.

The car didn't stop. It didn't even slow down until they approached Richmond, and then, to her surprise, she realised that they really were pulling into the car park of a pub by the river. When she threw the passenger door open and stumbled out, she could hear the sound of people chattering and laughing coming from the open windows.

The stranger got out from behind the wheel and stood watching her in silence. 'You've never done anything like this before, have you?' he asked at last.

Chloe shook her head.

'How did you feel during the drive?'

'Scared,' she admitted.

'Excited too?'

'A little.'

He took a step towards her. 'And are you still excited?'

She stared at him, seeing the desire in his eyes and knowing that he wanted her. 'Yes.'

Reaching out, he pushed her hair back behind her ears and stroked the side of her neck. 'Carlos was right, you're lovely.'

Chloe was stunned. 'What do you mean? Do you know Carlos?'

'I work for him. I'm sorry, Chloe. I'd love to spend the evening with you, but Carlos is waiting to take you back to London. Perhaps one day we'll have a chance to do this properly.' As he spoke, he slid a tiny card into her left hand, and she quickly put it into her shoulder bag, just before Carlos and Livia came out of the pub together.

'I told you she'd like Mike,' laughed Livia, kissing the blond man on both cheeks.

'It seems you were right,' said Carlos, staring intently at Chloe as she stood awkwardly by the car. 'I feel a little insulted that you were leaving me in order to pick up strange men, Chloe. Clearly I need to offer you more variety in your life. I had no idea quite how quickly you'd progressed.'

'I wasn't leaving you!' she protested. 'I'm a free agent. Why can't I make a date with a man if I want to?'

'You were leaving me. You have an overnight case in the car, and you had no intention of returning. Please remember, you are not a free agent. Behaviour like this is completely undisciplined. At the moment, your sexuality is being defined within the framework of my rules, and under my roof. I told you before that once you'd begun, there was no turning back. It seems you didn't believe me.'

'I was confused this morning. I needed time to think,' she protested

Carlos laughed. 'You didn't waste much time on thinking. I phoned Mike the moment you left the house with that little case of yours, and half an hour later you'd agreed to go out with a perfect stranger tonight. I admire your spirit of adventure. It's just a pity that in this particular instance you will have to be punished for it.'

'And punished now,' added Livia, satisfaction evident in her voice.

Chloe looked nervously at Carlos. 'What does she mean, now?'

'As you were so adventurous this morning, when Mike here tried to pick you up, we thought it would be a good idea if you went into this pub, became friendly with one of the men and then brought him outside and had sex with him.'

'I couldn't!' she protested.

'You don't have any choice,' said Carlos firmly. 'Hurry, it's nearly closing time.'

Chloe looked at Mike, and saw that he was watching her with interest. She realised that he was excited by what Carlos was proposing, and his excitement aroused her too. Without another word, she walked away from the three of them and into the crowded pub.

At the bar she ordered herself a glass of red wine, and as she sipped at it she glanced around the room, looking for likely men. After only a few minutes she made eye contact with a young man of about her own age sitting on the opposite side of the room with a group of friends.

He had dark-brown curly hair, and green eyes which brightened with interest when she looked his way. When he got to his feet and walked over to the bar, Chloe felt a buzz of excitement.

'On your own?' he asked casually, ordering himself a pint of beer.

'Yes. I finished work late and wanted to unwind before I went home.'

He glanced at her left hand. 'No husband, I take it?'

Chloe laughed. 'No attachments at all. I'm a free spirit.' She was amazed at how much she was beginning to enjoy herself.

'That's the kind of girl I like. My name's Jamie, what's yours?'

'Jemma,' she lied. It suddenly seemed important that Jamie never knew the real her.

'Hi, Jemma. Let me get you another glass of wine.'

'What about your friends?' she asked, seeing them watching what was happening.

'They're just leaving. I'm a free spirit too. There's no one waiting at home for me.'

Chloe looked straight into his eyes and smiled provocatively. 'That's lucky.'

He smiled back at her. 'My thoughts exactly.'

For the next five minutes they chatted idly about inconsequential things, and all the time Chloe was flirting with him. She touched him lightly on the arm to emphasise a point, tucked her hair behind her ears as she listened to him talking, and the sexual tension between them grew until she thought it must be obvious to everyone nearby.

'Let's go,' he said impatiently, the moment she'd finished her wine. 'My car's outside. I'll run you home.'

'Fine,' she agreed, sliding off the bar stool. As they walked out of the pub, he put an arm round her waist and slid his hand upwards until his fingers were brushing against her breast through the thin cotton of her dress.

The car park was only dimly lit, but Chloe was very aware that Carlos, Livia and Mike were sitting somewhere in the darkness, watching from their cars. If anything, their presence increased her excitement, and when Jamie bent his head to kiss her, she wound her arms round his neck and pulled him close to her.

'Let's do it now,' she whispered urgently.

'Now?' He drew his head back and looked at her in surprise. 'We can't. I only live five minutes away. Come back to my flat.'

She looked into his green eyes and knew, from the expression in them, that she was going to be able to get him to do what she wanted. 'I don't want to wait five minutes,' she whispered. 'Come on, let's go over here. No one will see us in those bushes.'

'What about the lights from the car park?' he asked huskily, letting her pull him along.

'They don't reach this far. Here, this will do. Quickly. I want you now.' Her hands were fumbling at his belt, unfastening his zip and releasing his erection, which sprang free with impressive urgency.

They were both breathing heavily, and Jamie guided her until her back was against a tree, then lifted her skirt up round her hips and pushed a hand between her thighs. He started to rub her through her panties, and within seconds she was soaking wet, moaning as the first sparks of pleasure flared behind her swollen clitoris.

Impatiently he tugged her panties down to her ankles. When she'd stepped out of them he lifted her legs up until they were round his waist and then thrust straight into her, his hands cupped beneath her buttocks to help her keep her balance.

Gasping with excitement, Chloe managed to undo the buttons at the top of her dress, and Jamie immediately bent his head and began to suck on her rigid nipples. Uttering tiny moans, she jerked her hips upwards, enabling him to penetrate her even more deeply.

Jamie movements were rough, and as she approached her climax he closed his mouth around her right nipple and bit it hard. Her whole body went rigid for a moment, and then her orgasm crashed down on her and her body twisted in paroxysms of pleasure.

She was vaguely aware that she was sobbing with delight, and that the sounds must be audible to everyone in the car park, but she didn't care. To have such power over a man she'd only just met was an intoxicating experience, and she wanted it to go on for ever.

Jamie lasted a long time, controlling himself until she managed a second orgasm, and then he too moaned loudly, his hips jerked in a frantic spasm and finally it was over.

As he helped her put her feet to the ground, their bodies were abruptly illuminated by a pair of car headlights being switched on. Both of them froze, their clothing in complete disarray, and Jamie moved quickly in front of Chloe.

A ripple of applause came from the direction of the car park, and then Carlos spoke, his voice carrying to them all too clearly. 'There's no need to protect her modesty, young man. She's won her bet now. You can go.'

Jamie looked at Chloe. 'Who is that? And what does he mean?'

All at once she felt completely wretched. 'I'm sorry,' she whispered, and with that she ran over the grass to where Carlos was waiting with the car.

'Well done! Most impressive. Get in the back now, it's time we returned to London.'

'He was nice,' added Livia. 'What was his name?'

'I didn't ask,' lied Chloe. 'Just a man I met at the bar.' Then she closed her eyes and pretended to go to sleep. She didn't want to discuss what had happened, or how it had made her feel, with anyone.

CHAPTER

10

To Chloe's surprise, nothing more was said about the evening once they arrived back home. Carlos simply said good night to her, then he and Livia went upstairs to bed.

It was difficult for her to settle after all that had happened. She kept replaying the scene with Jamie over and over in her mind, and the more she thought about it, the more aroused she became. When she heard Livia moaning and crying out with pleasure it was the last straw, and once again, she had to masturbate herself to orgasm before she could sleep.

The next morning she was certain that Carlos would want to talk to her before she left for work, but he didn't appear and she hardly saw him or Livia over the next few days. They were always in bed when she got up, and out when she arrived back in the evening.

'Are you okay?' asked Lizzie on the Friday as Chloe slammed her desk drawer shut.

'The florists say they can't do orange and white flowers for the dinner next month. They swear that we asked for various shades of pink and cream, which is rubbish.'

'I meant you personally,' said Lizzie. 'You haven't been yourself these past few days. It's not because some of the committee were difficult about you being at the top table with Carlos, is it?'

Chloe sighed. 'Of course not. I'm sorry, Lizzie. I feel a bit on edge at the moment. I've no idea why.'

'Sounds like love to me!'

'I wish I could tell you how wrong you are,' said Chloe.

Lizzie looked at her with concern. 'Why can't you tell me? I'm your friend; that's what friends are for, listening when there are problems. It's got something to do with Carlos Rocca, hasn't it?'

Running her hands through her hair, Chloe tried to ease some of the tension out of her neck and shoulders. 'In a way, yes, but the real problem is me.'

'In what way?'

'I don't know who or what I am any more.'

'Listen to me,' said Lizzie urgently. 'You're basically a nice girl, with unusually high standards for this day and age. There's nothing wrong with that. Innocence isn't a crime, and don't let Carlos or anyone else make you think otherwise.'

Chloe didn't know whether to laugh or cry. 'That's a very nice thing to say, but you really don't know me at all, Lizzie. The trouble is, neither do I.'

'Of course you do. Trust your instincts and you can't go wrong.'

Chloe nodded and picked up the phone. It was because she'd allowed herself to trust her instincts and go along with what Carlos suggested that she was so confused. Sensible Chloe, the girl who'd been a novice nun in Rio de Janeiro, would never have had sex with Jamie in the open air, or used Felipe in the way that she had. It was a different Chloe who was now living in Carlos's house, and her instincts were far from innocent.

*

Carlos lay naked on the bed, watching Livia dressing. He smiled to himself as she pulled on her scarlet thong, wincing as the material slid between her buttocks and pressed against the opening to her anus.

'You really hurt me this afternoon,' she complained.

'Nonsense, you know you enjoy it.'

She glanced at him, her dark-brown eyes puzzled. 'I don't always understand why I enjoy it.'

Her lover shrugged. 'I hope you're not going to start analysing your responses at this late stage in our relationship. Watching Chloe struggle to come to terms with what she really likes is fascinating. I know you too well to find a similar conflict in you intriguing.'

He knew that Livia would recognise his words for the warning they were meant to be. He enjoyed her because of her intense sexuality, and because she wasn't restricted by any sense of right or wrong. If Livia enjoyed something, then she did it, regardless of the consequences. It was an uncomplicated relationship, and he intended to keep it that way.

'Chloe is an interesting diversion. You know how much I enjoy corrupting innocence,' he continued as Livia dressed in silence. 'You and she are complete opposites, and that's what I find exciting. I don't want you to try and copy her. I want you to help me make her like you.'

Livia stared at his reflection in the mirror. 'And then what? Once you've totally corrupted her, what will you do with her? Abandon her?'

'I hadn't thought about it,' he said with total honesty. 'Once she's completed the discipline, then I imagine that we'll part company. You and I may see her from time to time, at some of our parties perhaps, but that's all.'

'I suppose I should feel sorry for her, but I don't.'

'That's because you're uncomfortable around her. For some reason, innocence makes you feel guilty.'

Livia put on her dress and looked away from the mirror. There were times when she hated Carlos, because he knew her too well. 'I think you're making a mistake ignoring Chloe like this. She might decide to find somewhere else to live if she thinks you've lost interest.'

'I enjoy keeping her on edge. Besides, I shall speak to her this evening. I have to; tomorrow night we have guests for dinner, and I intend Chloe to be there.'

Livia wasn't pleased. 'She can't come, it will make the numbers uneven.'

'I've invited Mike along to balance that out. We know she liked him; it should make the evening all the more interesting.'

'She might spoil things. Suppose she objects to what goes on, tries to leave the party before it ends or . . . ?'

'If you no longer trust my judgement, then perhaps you should think carefully about whether or not you wish to stay here with me, Livia. Maybe you'd be happier back in Rio?' he said coldly.

Realising that she'd gone too far, Livia subdued her natural reaction, which was to shout at him in fury, and instead tried to placate him. She certainly didn't want to be sent back to Rio de Janeiro, leaving him alone with Chloe. 'I'm sorry,' she apologised. 'It's only that I enjoy our dinner parties so much, and I'm afraid she might spoil this one.'

Getting up off the bed, Carlos walked over to Livia and caught hold of her long blond hair, pulling her head back sharply. 'Trust me, Chloe will make this one of the best dinner parties we've ever had,' he said softly. Livia kept very still. He licked delicately at the soft skin at the base of her throat before releasing her.

'I do trust you,' she assured him.

'I hope that's true, Livia. Trust is something that's very important to me.'

After he'd gone to shower, Livia touched the place on her neck where his tongue had caressed her skin, and shivered. She knew that she must be more careful in the future. If Carlos thought that she was becoming too jealous of Chloe, he would dismiss her from his life, and that was something she wasn't prepared to accept. Somehow she had to ensure that it was Chloe who vanished, and she was ready to go to any lengths to make sure that happened.

'We haven't seen much of you these past few days, Chloe,' remarked Carlos as the three of them sat down to eat that evening. 'I apologise for that.'

'I don't expect you to be here for me!' laughed Chloe. 'I've been busy at work, and you've been out a lot in the evenings.'

'Livia and I enjoyed the evening at Richmond,' he continued smoothly, and she felt herself beginning to blush. 'I wonder if that man is still searching for the girl who seduced him so efficiently.'

'Do you wish you could see him again, Chloe?' asked Livia, draining her wine glass and immediately refilling it.

'No! I'd die of shame.'

Carlos raised an eyebrow. 'Why? You didn't do anything wrong. From what I could see of it, you both gained a great deal of pleasure from the experience.'

'It's not the way I'd normally have behaved.'

He gave a thin smile. 'I know, I made you do it.'

'Well you did,' retorted Chloe hotly. 'It was my punishment, remember?'

'It looked more like a reward to me. However, that's history now. We're having a dinner party here tomorrow night. I hope you're free to come?'

Chloe hesitated. 'Well, I . . .'

Livia looked sharply at her. 'Don't you want to meet some of our friends?'

'It isn't that. It's just that I'm not used to that kind of thing, and I don't have anything suitable to wear. You always look so glamorous, Livia. It's kind of you to ask me but I'd be like a fish out of water.'

'You'll fit in perfectly. You and Livia can go shopping for a suitable dress tomorrow afternoon,' declared Carlos firmly. 'Don't worry about not knowing anyone, Chloe. Mike will be there.'

She stared at him. 'Mike?'

'Yes. I take it you haven't forgotten him already?'

'Of course not, but I hadn't expected to see him again.'

'You were wrong. Mike's looking forward to the evening. Now, if you girls will excuse me, I have some business to attend to. If I don't see you before, we'll meet up tomorrow evening at seven-thirty in my study, Chloe,' he concluded. With that he left.

Livia raised her glass to Chloe. 'Here's to happy shopping tomorrow!'

'To happy shopping,' agreed Chloe, raising her glass of water, but as Livia gave an unamused laugh, she had the uneasy feeling that it wasn't going to be a happy experience at all.

Chloe looked at her reflection in the mirror of the changing room with utter disbelief. 'I can't wear that!' she told the watching Livia.

'Why not?'

'Because it isn't me.'

Livia tapped the toe of her right shoe against the floor in irritation. 'You've been saying that for the past three hours, every time I pick out something for you to wear, in fact. The problem is, the things that you think *are* you would make you look ridiculously out of place tonight.'

Chloe stared at herself once more. The strapless black

89

and red dress fitted her like a second skin, clinging to every curve. It made her look more voluptuous than she really was, and showed far more cleavage than she felt comfortable revealing.

'It's too obviously sexy,' she explained. 'I think clothes that cover you up are more erotic than things like this. This doesn't give me any sense of mystery.'

'If you want to mystify people tonight, wear your nun's habit,' snapped Livia. 'I'm tired of this. If you want to choose something boring then go ahead, just don't blame me when Carlos doesn't like it.'

'I won't. Anyway, I think he will like that blue dress I tried on earlier. You know, the one that's got transparent sleeves and a slashed skirt.'

Livia shrugged with an eloquence that only she could achieve with such a small gesture. 'Then buy it.'

'You don't like it?'

The blond-haired girl pulled a face. 'I wouldn't be seen dead in it, but we're not alike, you and I, so that doesn't mean anything.'

When Livia left the changing room, Chloe felt a sense of triumph. They weren't alike, which was why having Livia try to choose a dress for her had been such a disaster. Taking the blue dress over to the till, she knew that she'd made the right choice. This dress was elegant and discreetly sexy. It would suit her, and if Carlos didn't like it, that was too bad.

'What are you wearing tonight?' she asked a silent and sullen Livia as they took a taxi back to the house.

'A pink Versace dress that Carlos bought me last month. It's his favourite.'

'Lucky you.'

Livia glanced sideways at her. 'You think so?'

'Well, it can't be bad, having a lover who buys you designer dresses and—'

'And what?'

Chloe felt confused. 'Sorry.'

'What else is it about my life with Carlos that makes you think I'm lucky?'

Chloe couldn't understand why Livia was suddenly on the defensive. 'He loves you,' she said slowly. 'Surely that feels good?'

Livia gave her a pitying glance. 'He doesn't know the meaning of the word love. Surely you know that by now?'

Chloe was relieved that at that moment the taxi drew up outside the house, and she was able to escape up to her room. It was obvious that Livia felt antagonistic towards her, but she couldn't imagine why. Livia wasn't the one being humiliated and disciplined. She was the one sharing Carlos's bed and most private thoughts. If anything, it should be Chloe resenting Livia.

Putting the other girl's words to the back of her mind, she started thinking about the dinner party, and what it would be like to see Mike again.

CHAPTER

11

It was seven-twenty, and Chloe was just checking herself in the mirror when she heard a light tap at the bedroom door. Guessing that it was Livia, coming to run a critical eye over her appearance, she murmured a weary 'Come in,' and then continued studying her reflection.

'Very nice,' said Carlos approvingly. 'A little more modest than I'd expected, but highly suitable for an ex-nun.'

Chloe turned to look at him. 'You like it then?'

He nodded. 'Yes. Livia told me she'd had problems with you, but I think you made a good choice. Sometimes it's more erotic to reveal only a little of yourself at the beginning of an evening.'

Chloe, who had no intention of revealing more of herself at any stage, was elated. So much for Livia's expertise. 'I'd hardly call this revealing very little of myself,' she said with a laugh. 'When I move, this dress is split to the thigh on one side.'

Carlos nodded. 'True, but you're wearing tights under it. Bare legs would have been sexier. Never mind. I wanted to make a suggestion to you. Some of tonight's guests might well be interested in your charity. You must see if you can persuade them to make donations.'

'I couldn't possibly!' exclaimed Chloe in horror. 'Not tonight, it's a social occasion. They'd think me very rude.'

He gave a half-smile. 'That rather depends on how you try to persuade them. They might enjoy it. Think about it, Chloe. Now I must go and join my guests. I hope tonight is fun for you.'

As he closed the door behind him, Chloe tried not to think about what Carlos might have meant by his suggestion. Taking a deep breath, she sprayed on some Arpège, which she'd bought that afternoon, and went to join him and his guests.

Everyone was gathered in the study, chattering away loudly, but as Chloe walked in, their voices slowly stopped and they all turned to look at her. Feeling incredibly self-conscious, she walked across the thick carpet to where Carlos was waiting by the drinks cabinet. 'I hope I'm not late,' she murmured.

'Not at all. What would you like to drink?'

'Bacardi and Coke, please.' His blue eyes locked on to her grey ones and for a few seconds it felt as though they were the only two people in the room, then he put a hand on her shoulder and guided her towards his guests.

'Livia, make Chloe her drink, please. Chloe, I want you to meet Natasha and Christopher. Christopher lived in Brazil for a few years, it's where we met.'

Christopher, who looked as though he probably had some Brazilian blood in him, quickly started asking Chloe questions about her time in Rio de Janeiro, questions which she tried to avoid because the last thing she wanted to do at this stage of the evening was mention that she'd once been a nun.

Natasha was a pretty, auburn-haired young girl, wearing a brown leather dress that clung to her body like a second skin. A zip ran down the front of the dress, and it had two fastenings. The bottom one was open to just below her crotch and the top one was pulled down to reveal the tops of her small but beautifully rounded creamy breasts.

When Livia brought Chloe's drink over, she also brought another couple with her, introducing them as Verity and Anthony. It seemed difficult for Anthony to take his eyes off Natasha, which surprised Chloe because Verity was a stunning dusky beauty dressed in a long, tight-fitting plum-coloured dress that was completely transparent and made no secret of the fact that she wasn't wearing any underwear.

As Christopher began talking about his own time in Brazil, Chloe's attention wandered for a moment, and it was only then that she noticed a familiar figure standing quietly at the opposite side of the room. It was Mike. She felt herself start to flush at the memory of their drive to Richmond.

At that moment, a hand touched her lightly on the nape of her neck. 'Are you pleased to see Mike?' whispered Carlos. She didn't answer, and his fingers tightened on the delicate flesh hidden by her curly dark hair. His grip became uncomfortable, and she knew that she'd have to reply.

'I don't know,' she whispered.

'I know!' laughed Carlos, and then he lifted her hair up and kissed the nape of her neck before guiding everyone in to dinner.

As they sat down, Livia introduced Chloe to the third couple who were making up the dinner party, a blond-haired girl called Fiona, who was wearing a black lace mini-dress, and her partner Mehrdad, an Iranian businessman. Mike was seated on Chloe's right-hand side and Christopher on her left, which meant that there was no shortage of conversation during the meal.

By the time the desserts were served, everyone except for Chloe and Carlos had drunk a lot of wine. Chloe had drunk more than she usually did, but she was keenly aware of the fact that Carlos had drunk very little. She sensed that he'd done this deliberately, and it made her uneasy.

Mike draped an arm along the back of her chair and put his head close to hers. 'When I watched you with that guy from the pub the other night, I nearly went out of my mind with frustration,' he whispered. 'All I kept thinking was "I wish that was me".'

'All *I* kept thinking was "Why on earth am I doing this?"' replied Chloe.

'You loved it,' said Mike, his voice thickening with desire. 'I could see that you did, we could all tell. Even Carlos was surprised at how enthusiastic you were. Later on, how about you and I slip out into the garden?' As he spoke, his left hand began to stroke her knee, and then his fingers slid higher up her leg until he was tickling the top of her inner thigh.

Chloe felt her breath start to quicken, and she pushed his hand away. 'Don't, Mike, please. I'm not like that really. You don't understand.'

'Of course I do. Carlos told me all about you. How you used to be a nun, and wanted someone to teach you about sensuality and so he—'

'Is that what he said?' asked Chloe. She was so astonished that her voice was far louder than she'd intended, and everyone at the table looked at her in surprise. Horrified, she fell silent. When Mike's hand began to roam over her leg again she let it stay there, while Carlos watched her thoughtfully from the end of the table.

It was only while they were drinking coffee in the drawing room that Chloe noticed that Livia was flirting with Natasha. She kept pulling on the top zip fastener of the girl's leather dress, and at one stage she stroked the exposed tops of Natasha's breasts with her fingers. Carlos appeared totally untroubled, but Christopher seemed less than pleased.

Chloe couldn't understand why the other guests didn't take any notice of what was happening, and when the two girls got up and left the room together, no one said a word. Instead they all continued talking among themselves.

However, the atmosphere changed, and now Christopher pulled Fiona on to his lap, and the two of them started to kiss passionately, while Mehrdad watched impassively, his black eyes occasionally flicking over to where Chloe was sitting talking to Mike.

Carlos watched them all, and when Mehrdad got up to move across to Chloe, he spoke. 'Chloe, you haven't told my friends about your charity work yet.'

'There's nothing to say,' muttered Chloe, trying to push Mike's hand away as his fingers reached the top of her thighs.

'Of course there is. Well, if you're shy, I'll tell them for you. Chloe supports a very worthy charity connected with her time as a nun in Rio de Janeiro.' At the word 'nun', all the men in the room stopped what they were doing and stared at Chloe in surprise. 'She's always on the lookout for wealthy supporters of this charity, so if by tomorrow morning any of you feel that you'd like to make one or indeed regular donations, then don't forget to ask her for the details. Now, Chloe, I think it's time we all went upstairs, don't you?'

Chloe sat very still. She knew that this was a very important moment in their relationship, and the entire concept of 'the discipline'. No matter how much Carlos had made it seem that she was the same as the other guests here tonight, she wasn't. She was here as part of her training, and now he was telling her that it was time to take yet another step forward into his darkly erotic world.

The men continued to watch her silently, their eyes bright with excited anticipation, and even Fiona seemed aroused. Only Verity, sitting alone in a large leather chair, showed no interest. The atmosphere was heavy with sexual tension, and Chloe was aware that there was a clock in the room, and the seconds were slowly ticking away as she tried to decide what to do.

'Chloe?' His voice was gentle, but she knew that Carlos was losing patience.

Her body felt hot and tight, and as Mike's fingers continued to tease between her thighs she felt herself growing increasingly damp. She knew then that she did want to go upstairs, and to continue the journey that Carlos was taking her on. 'Yes,' she said quietly. 'I think it is time.'

Standing up, Carlos reached out a hand and helped Chloe to her feet. 'You won't regret it,' he promised her as he led her from the room.

Livia looked down at Natasha, lying spreadeagled on the large circular bed of the main guest room, and Natasha stared back at her. The auburn-haired girl was breathing rapidly, the swell of her breasts rising and falling within the confines of her tight leather dress.

The bottom end of the zip had been pulled up, leaving her totally exposed below the waist, but above it she was still trapped, and her breasts were aching as they pressed against the tight leather covering.

When the door opened and some of the guests came into the room, Livia didn't even glance at them, but Natasha did. Her swollen, hot body moved on the silken bed covering as her light-green eyes searched for Chris but, as she'd half expected, he wasn't there. Neither was Verity.

Anthony was there though, and she could see from the look on his face how much he wanted her. With a small smile of satisfaction, she waited for Livia to continue, her arousal increased by Anthony's presence.

As Livia lowered her head and ran her tongue between Natasha's outer sex lips, and Natasha started to squirm helplessly as her skin began to prickle and her nipples hardened again, Carlos caught hold of Fiona and deftly removed her black lace mini-dress.

Natasha heard Fiona squeal in protest, but then she lost sight of her, and now all she could think about was what Livia was doing to her. The Brazilian beauty was opening her up with her hands, teasing her throbbing clitoris with the tip of one finger to encourage her to swell even more, and then, as Natasha's internal muscles contracted sharply in an orgasm, Livia slipped something cool and smooth inside her.

Natasha made a sound of protest, struggling to sit upright, but Livia pressed her back against the bed. 'It's only love balls,' she explained. 'They'll increase the pleasure, keep you aroused there while I concentrate on your breasts.' She then pressed the palm of one hand against Natasha's vulva, and immediately an ache began deep inside her. She longed for more stimulation so that she could climax, but instead Livia took her hand away and very slowly began to unzip the top of Natasha's dress.

Natasha gasped as unseen hands caught hold of her legs, spreading them wide apart, and then they were being fastened with cord to buckles on the edge of the bed, leaving her helpless. She wanted to know who was tying her up, but Livia was crouched above her, blocking her view.

When the zip was pulled right down to Natasha's waist, and her throbbing breasts with their rigid nipples were finally freed, the dress fell off, and every centimetre of her skin was uncovered.

'Enjoying yourself?' asked Livia, and when Natasha moaned with delight, Livia caught hold of one of her nipples and pinched it tightly between finger and thumb. The pain caught Natasha by surprise, and she cried out, but then Livia started to lick the throbbing tip and the pain was replaced by waves of pleasure.

'Tighten your internal muscles,' whispered Livia. 'If you do that now, the love balls will help you climax.' Moaning softly to herself, Natasha did as Livia suggested. Immediately she felt the cool globes caressing the inner walls of her vagina, touching the delicate nerve endings of the G-spot. She moved her hips as much as she could, trying to increase the pressure within her, but Livia only slapped her across her bare belly and then nipped her already sore nipple with her teeth.

Natasha wasn't sure if she liked that or not, and she tried to twist her torso away from Livia, but the blonde was far stronger than she was. As she held Natasha down with one hand, she gently licked at the abused nipple again, this time teasing it with the tip of her tongue.

The combination of sensations, coupled with the sound of heavy breathing from the watching guests, meant that Natasha's body was swamped by a massive orgasm, making her cry out with shame and delight as every muscle spasmed in abandoned pleasure.

Afterwards, as she lay, sweat-streaked and tousled, her body still shaking slightly, Livia quickly got off the bed, slipped out of her backless pink silk dress and then lay on top of the other girl's quivering body.

Natasha felt Livia's hips press against hers and groaned with delight as their pubic mounds ground together, causing tendrils of pleasure to snake through her. Instinctively she reached up with her hands and began to stroke Livia's breasts, which made the Brazilian girl move her body faster, until the pair of them climaxed together in a sharp, sweet moment of release.

As Livia rolled off her, Natasha looked around the room. Anthony was standing to the side of the bed, and when he caught her eye he moistened his lips with the tip of his tongue and then made a movement towards her.

'You want her, Anthony?' asked Carlos.

'You know I do.'

Natasha shivered with excitement at his words.

'Then take her into the next room. All that you need is there, waiting for you. Be careful, though. Natasha has never played the slave girl before, have you, Tasha?'

Her mouth went dry as she remembered the last time she and Christopher had been to one of Carlos's dinner parties. That time another of the guests had taken the role of slave girl to some of the men there, and she could still recall it all very vividly. At least it would be different from her life with Christopher, she thought, and then her legs were released and Anthony hustled her naked off the bed.

It was only when she reached the door, and looked back for one final glance at Livia, that Natasha saw with surprise what had happened to Fiona, despite the fact that Mehrdad was there with her.

'Come on,' said Anthony urgently. 'I can't wait much longer,' and with that he took her out of the room and away from the other guests, leaving them to continue their games without her.

Chloe, who had watched the entire scene in silence, was also surprised by what had happened to Fiona. Once Carlos had removed the blonde's black dress, he'd put her in a heavy leather suit, with shoulder straps and thick leather rings around her breasts, rings which were then pulled up high, leaving the undersides exposed. A double strip of leather hung from the centre of the breast rings down each side of her stomach before separating into leg holes, while a wide band of leather was passed between her thighs, with holes for her front and rear openings. At the back this strip was looped into another single leather band that went up the middle of her back where it joined the shoulder straps.

All the straps were adjusted to press tightly against Fiona's body, and then her hands were tied behind her back and she was secured to a small ring set in the wall opposite the bed. This meant that she could watch everything that was happening, but was helpless to do anything herself.

Carlos, who saw the puzzlement in Chloe's eyes, ran a hand casually over the tethered blond girl's up-thrust breasts. 'She's for later. Watching will make her all the keener, isn't that right, Mehrdad?'

Mehrdad glanced briefly at his wife and nodded. It seemed that her plight was of no interest to him at all, but Chloe could tell that in fact the Iranian was still watching Fiona closely.

'Isn't anyone else going to join me?' asked Livia, lying on her side on the bed.

'Of course they are,' replied Carlos. 'Mike, why don't you, Mehrdad and Chloe have some fun along with Livia now. I'll watch with Fiona. I'm sure she'd like a little company.'

'Where are Christopher and Verity?' asked Chloe quietly.

'Christopher has different needs from the other men here. Fortunately Verity likes to cater to them for him. Off you go then, Chloe. Enjoy yourself, and remember that I'm watching you. I expect you to keep my guests well entertained. Don't disappoint me.'

Mehrdad was already naked on the bed with Livia, and

Mike was busy taking off his clothes, but Chloe felt rooted to the spot. 'I don't know if I can,' she whispered.

'Of course you can. You saw how much Natasha enjoyed herself, and it aroused you. Your body needs satisfaction, I can tell.'

'But not with strangers, and in front of you, it's—'

'It's what I'm demanding of you,' he reminded her. 'Remember that, and don't forget that your charity will do well out of this too. Mehrdad will give generously if you please him.'

Chloe didn't take any notice of his last sentence. She was doing this because she needed to know more about the dark world that Carlos inhabited, and also because she had a feeling that Livia was hoping she'd fail. Slowly she removed her blue dress, and then Mike came over and helped her out of her underwear until she was finally naked. Very slowly, his hand clasping her wrist tightly, he drew her over to the bed.

'I've been wanting to pleasure you for a very long time,' he murmured. Then he was pressing her backwards until she was lying naked in the middle of the bed, while Carlos watched from the shadows, his hands occasionally moving over exposed areas of flesh on the tethered Fiona's body as she whimpered with frustration.

For Carlos, this was going to be a very interesting evening, because it would be the biggest test so far of Chloe's willingness to be guided by him and his desires.

CHAPTER

12

When Mike began to kiss Chloe's neck and shoulders, she relaxed against the silk bed covering, relishing the feel of the material against her bare flesh. She was vaguely aware that Livia was lying near her, moaning softly as Mehrdad's hands began to stroke her heavy breasts and his tongue lapped at her dark nipples.

The sounds of Livia's excitement increased Chloe's own desire and she thrust her hips upwards towards Mike, so that their bodies were closer together. Reaching between her thighs, he cupped her vulva with the palm of his hand, pressing firmly against her until she felt the tension growing in her lower belly. It was a delicious sensation, and when he ran his tongue over her ribs, just below her left breast, while at the same time increasing the pressure between her thighs, she groaned aloud with pleasure.

Next to her, Livia was moving more and more frantically, her body occasionally touching Chloe's as Mehrdad continued to arouse her before bringing her to a short, sharp orgasm that made her hips arch off the bed.

Realising what had happened, Chloe grew desperate for a climax herself, and began to make tiny pleading noises that made Mike smile. 'Ready?' he asked softly, and when she nodded, he put his head between her thighs and ran his tongue backwards and forwards over her damp, swollen clitoris in long, sweeping motions that immediately triggered her moment of release, and her body shook violently as her muscles contracted with pleasure.

As she lay with her eyes closed, her breathing gradually slowing, she became aware that she was being moved around the bed, and that her arms and legs were being stretched apart until she was spreadeagled in an X shape. Opening her eyes, she struggled to sit up, but she was too late to stop the other three from fastening her securely to the bed, just as Natasha had been fastened earlier.

This was something she didn't want, to be at the mercy of relative strangers with Carlos watching her, but there was nothing she could do about it now and so she lay silently, waiting to see what they intended to do.

Although her wrists were tied with cord looped into metal rings, her legs were held apart by a length of wooden board that was fastened to her ankles with metal cuffs. This meant that no matter what happened, she couldn't close her legs, and remained open and exposed to them all the time.

'What's the matter?' asked Livia softly, kneeling on the bed next to Chloe. 'You look nervous. We aren't going to hurt you. This evening is for pleasure.'

'I don't like what you've done to my legs,' retorted Chloe.

'It's what Carlos wanted. I'm sure you want to make him happy, don't you?'

Chloe swallowed nervously. 'I know that I must obey him, it's part of the discipline,' she murmured.

Mehrdad, who was standing beside the bed, raised his eyebrows. 'So, you too are trying to learn the discipline. That's interesting. Fiona tried once, before I knew her, but she failed, didn't you, darling?' and he turned to look at his wife.

Chloe looked at her too. Carlos was tweaking one of her nipples between a finger and thumb, and the other nipple was standing out from her swollen breasts, a crimson, pointed little tip that looked both sore and aroused. She was making tiny sounds of protests, but at the same time straining frantically towards Carlos for further stimulation, a movement that he was totally ignoring.

'She lacked courage,' explained Mehrdad, apparently still unconcerned by his wife's plight, and then he took a small jar from Mike and moved round to the end of the bed. 'Livia brought this over with her from Rio de Janeiro,' he explained, removing the lid. 'It's a very special cream, as you'll soon discover.'

Slowly, sensuously, he licked the tip of his middle finger and then dipped it into the jar before bending over the tethered Chloe and spreading a tiny amount of the cream on her right nipple. It felt cool on her skin and she wondered what all the fuss was about, but then as the seconds passed the sensation changed.

At first her nipple began to prickle lightly, but the prickles quickly changed to strong tingling sensations and she felt her nipple swelling as the strange burning heat that was spreading through it stimulated the nerve endings.

Her eyes widened in surprise, then, when the sensation continued to grow in intensity, she tried to move her upper body around a little, to ease the terrible throbbing that was making her nipple so engorged.

'A little on the other one now, I think,' said Livia, her eyes sparkling.

'No!' protested Chloe, not wanting to experience the same sensation again, but she saw Carlos nod at Mehrdad, and deftly he spread some more of the cream on to the other nipple. This time Chloe wasn't fooled by the initial coolness, and as the warm, tingling feelings grew she lay very still, hoping that this might be better than moving around.

Mike, Mehrdad and Livia watched her closely, and soon Chloe gave up all resistance to the sensations and began to try and thrust her cruelly aroused nipples upwards, desperate for someone to caress them.

It was Mehrdad who bent over her this time, drawing one of the nipples into his mouth and grazing the frantic tip with his teeth. Chloe's body had never felt so aroused, so alive, and within seconds she was climaxing. She groaned in an agony of release and desperation because, despite the climax, her nipples continued to throb.

As her upper torso twisted restlessly within its bonds, Mehrdad moved his hand lower down her body. Realising what he intended to do, Chloe cried out in protest again, but once more Carlos overruled her, and as the deceptively cool ointment was spread over her already swollen clitoris, Chloe braced herself for what was to come.

Within seconds the cream took effect, and she could feel herself opening up between her thighs, her clitoris swelling and her sex lips blooming as her frantic body screamed for release from its state of ecstatic delirium.

Pushing Mehrdad out of the way, Mike stroked the side of her tight, hard, swollen nub of pleasure, and this time as another orgasm tore through her she felt as though her body was going to split in two.

The orgasm seemed endless, but finally it peaked and her muscles started to relax a little as the all-consuming hot pleasure began to die down. Immediately, Mike touched her clitoris again, rubbing around its base in a circular motion. Because of the effect of Livia's cream, Chloe was immediately consumed by another frighteningly intense orgasm, an orgasm so fierce that the spasms made all her muscles ache.

'Wasn't that good?' asked Livia when Chloe's body was at last still again.

Chloe stared at her, feeling the sweat between her breasts, and her own juices between her parted thighs. 'It was too much,' she murmured.

'But we've only just begun!' laughed Livia, and when Chloe opened her mouth in protest, the Brazilian girl spread some cream around her lips, which quickly swelled and began to throb, while her helplessly wanton body responded by starting to crave yet more satisfaction.

Her breasts grew heavy, there was a tugging sensation deep within her belly and her clitoris felt hard and hot again. 'You want another climax, don't you?' whispered Livia. 'Admit it, Chloe. There's no shame in it. I'm the same when I use the cream.'

As her breathing quickened and desire raged through her, Chloe couldn't see the point in denying it. 'Yes!' she cried. 'Yes, I need to come again.'

'Leave a vibrator inside her,' said Livia to Mike. 'She won't be able to take it out, and she'll keep coming until we remove it.'

'No, that's not what I want,' protested Chloe.

Carlos moved slightly in the shadows. 'It's what I want,' he said firmly. 'Will you do what I want, Chloe, or have you changed your mind? Remember, I can help you reach heights of ecstasy you'd never imagined existed.'

Chloe's body was so overstimulated, so needy, that she was past caring now, and anyway she knew that Carlos was right. For better or for worse, she was entering a whole new world.

'All right,' she agreed, and immediately Mehrdad slid a long, slim vibrator deep inside her damp entrance and then switched it on. Almost as soon as the vibrations began, she started to climax again.

'You can watch us while the vibrator pleasures you,' said Livia. Mike lay down on the side of the bed, with his feet on the floor, then, once Livia was impaled on him, her body bent low across his, Mehrdad pushed himself roughly inside her rectum.

Lost in a world of seemingly endless orgasms, where one climax began almost as soon the previous one had finished, Chloe's mind was aroused as much as her body by the sight of Livia being possessed by two men at once, trapped between them as they took their pleasure with an almost careless disregard for hers.

It seemed to be an eternity before all three of them were satisfied, and only when Livia slid to the floor did Mehrdad walk round to the end of the bed and remove the vibrator from inside Chloe.

As he slid it out of her, it felt as though he was drawing her insides out with it, and she shivered at the strange sensation, which was a mixture of relief and loss.

'I think you've nearly had enough for one evening, but we can't leave you like this,' said Mehrdad, stroking her belly for a moment, until she started to quiver with pleasure again. 'What do you want us to do, Carlos?'

Chloe lifted her head up off the bed as far as she could and tried to make out the expression on Carlos's face, but he was still in the shadows and it was impossible. Tensely she waited to hear what he had to say.

At first he didn't reply, but the silence was suddenly broken by a gasping cry from Fiona, followed by soft sobs and whimpering. 'She's feeling frustrated,' explained Carlos casually. 'No doubt you will compensate her for this little ordeal later tonight, Mehrdad. In the mean time, I think that Chloe must be cooled down before the evening draws to an end.'

'I know just the way to do it!' exclaimed Livia, getting off the bed and walking slowly across the room to the door. 'I won't be gone long, Chloe. Don't worry!' she added as Chloe watched her helplessly.

'How do you feel?' asked Mike, brushing her breasts gently with the back of his fingers. Even this slight movement was enough to re-arouse her still overheated flesh, and her breath caught in her throat as her exhausted nerve endings began to flicker into life again.

'She's very aroused,' commented Mehrdad, sliding one slim finger inside her vagina and pressing upwards against her G-spot. 'Obviously the vibrator wasn't enough for her.'

'It was!' cried Chloe. 'It's not my fault. It's this cream of Livia's that's doing it. I don't want to keep coming like this, but I can't help it.'

'You love it,' said Carlos calmly. 'I can see it in your eyes, and in the way you move around. Look, Mehrdad, she's coming again.'

Chloe knew that he was right. As Mehrdad kept up the steady pressure with his finger, and Mike continued brushing the surface of her breasts, white lights began to flash behind her closed eyelids and again her body tightened, her flesh quickened and swelled and then all the sensations rushed together in a flooding moment of hot, wet relief, leaving her gasping for breath.

'What have you been doing?' asked Livia as she came back into the room, carrying a large ice bucket.

'Pleasuring Chloe, of course,' laughed Mike.

'Lucky Chloe.'

Chloe wasn't sure that this was true. She felt as though her body was on fire, and longed for the stimulation of her exhausted yet still demanding flesh to stop. At the same time, when she was left alone, her body felt bereft and Fiona's continuing cries of frustration were like a teasing echo of the way Chloe felt.

'This should help,' said Livia, placing the ice bucket on a bedside table. 'We'll all take ice cubes in our mouths and then use them on Chloe. Who wants to go first?'

'Me!' said Mike quickly, and Chloe watched as he picked an ice cube out of the bucket and slid it into his mouth. As he sucked briefly on it, he watched Chloe closely, and she trembled as she tried to imagine what it would feel like when the cube touched her scorching-hot skin.

Leaning towards her, Mike drew her right nipple and the surrounding flesh into his mouth and then sucked so that the ice cube moved over the entire surface. The contrast between the freezing ice and her hot, throbbing skin was almost unbearably shocking, and Chloe gave a small scream. As the coldness began to quench the burning ache in her breast, she heard herself half sobbing with gratitude.

Immediately Livia and Mehrdad joined in. Mehrdad attended to Chloe's left nipple and breast, while Livia put her head between Chloe's forcibly parted legs. Then, with exquisite care, she opened the other girl up and pushed the ice cube high inside her vagina with the tip of her tongue.

Chloe's hot and abused internal flesh jumped at the sudden cold invasion, and instinctively she tried to eject it, but the ice cube was already melting and proved impossible to move. 'You'll have to wait until it's melted, I'm afraid,' purred Livia. 'You're very hot in there. I think you need a little more ice.'

Chloe started to tremble because the contrast in sensations was proving arousing rather than soothing, but she didn't want Livia to know. However, Livia was too experienced to miss the tell-tale signs. She returned three times to the ice bucket, and every cube aroused Chloe even more.

Finally, when the fourth one was inserted into her, her belly began to quake and Livia immediately pressed the palm of her hand on the soft flesh just above Chloe's pubic hair line, so that her jangling nerves were stimulated even more.

With a helpless cry, Chloe gave herself over to the wonderful, mind-shattering orgasm that had been building steadily within her. As her head twisted and turned on the bed, Carlos watched her through narrowed blue eyes, his breathing quick and shallow.

Finally, Chloe's body was still. 'What now?' asked Livia.

'Untie her and remove the spreader board,' said Carlos. 'I think she needs some rest, unlike Fiona here, who's more than ready for some excitement.'

'I'll take Fiona back to our room,' said Mehrdad swiftly, but through half-closed eyes Chloe could see that although Carlos unfastened the blond girl, she was still in the leather harness when her husband led her away.

Mike helped Chloe sit upright, while Livia watched her with interest. 'I think you enjoyed yourself tonight,' she remarked.

'That's what you said I was supposed to do,' retorted Chloe, but she was still trembling slightly from everything that had happened to her.

'I'll take Chloe to her room,' said Carlos.

Livia frowned. 'I'm sure she knows the way.'

'What's the matter, don't you want to be left here alone with me?' asked Mike teasingly.

'I'm sure she'd love to spend some time with you,' remarked Carlos, and then he put an arm round Chloe's naked waist and began to lead her from the room.

'My dress!' she exclaimed.

'You can have that back tomorrow. Tonight is not a night for clothes.'

Feeling suddenly awkward, Chloe followed him along the passage towards her own room. On the way, they passed an open bedroom door. Inside she saw Christopher crawling round on the floor, a leather collar round his neck, while Verity stood over him striking him hard with a leather tawse. As she watched, Chloe heard him give a yelp of pain.

'It's all right,' said Carlos. 'That's what Christopher enjoys, and Verity is the perfect partner for him.'

'Is that what Natasha does for him too?' asked Chloe in surprise.

'Unfortunately for Christopher, no! That's why they both enjoy my little dinner parties so much. I've enjoyed this one as well. You exceeded all my expectations, Chloe. How fortunate for us that you decided not to remain a nun!'

Chloe felt herself blushing furiously. 'I was so ashamed,' she muttered.

'I think not, my little one. Surprised perhaps, and undoubtedly embarrassed, but not truly ashamed, or your body would not have responded as it did. I've trained you well. Mehrdad enjoyed himself hugely. I'm sure he'll be more than happy to make a generous donation to your charity.'

'Well, I'm not going to ask him to do that,' retorted Chloe. 'What happened here tonight has nothing to do with my work.'

'Did you remember all the time that I was watching you?' he asked quietly.

'Yes,' confessed Chloe.

'And did it excite you to know I was there?'

She hung her head, and he quickly put a hand under her chin and tilted it upwards. 'You must never be ashamed of what you do, never. Tell me the truth now. Did it excite you?'

'Yes, you know it did.'

He gave a small sigh of pleasure. 'Excellent,' he murmured, and then he was opening her bedroom door and standing back to let her go through. 'Sleep well, you must be exhausted.'

'Aren't you coming in with me?' she asked, and he laughed.

'I see you've taken my words to heart! No, not tonight. You need to rest, and I want to join Mehrdad and Fiona. I enjoy tormenting Fiona, because she failed me once before,' he added, his smile fading.

'What if I fail you?' asked Chloe.

'Then you'll leave and we'll never meet again, but you won't fail me. I know that now. Tomorrow, when everyone's gone, we'll discuss the charity dinner. Now sleep.' After he'd closed the door behind him, Chloe found that she only just had enough strength left to get into bed before she fell sound asleep.

CHAPTER

13

The following day, Chloe deliberately kept out of the way of everyone else in the house. In the morning she caught up with some office paperwork in her room, then went for a long walk. In the afternoon she went and saw a foreign film. Afterwards, when she was on her way back to Carlos's house, she realised she didn't have a clue what the film had been about, but at least it had kept her occupied. She didn't want to think about the night before, and she certainly didn't wish to meet any of the weekend guests.

By the time she got back, the house was quiet and she slipped into the kitchen to make herself a snack. As she started going through the cupboards, looking for some pasta, Carlos came in.

'What are you doing?'

'Making myself dinner.'

'Don't you want to eat with me tonight?'

Chloe turned to face him. 'I didn't know you were here. The house seemed deserted.'

'It's Mrs Clarke's evening off and Livia's visiting friends, but I stayed behind. I wanted to talk to you, as I think I mentioned last night.'

Chloe nodded. She couldn't help noticing how attractive

he was looking. He'd replaced his usual formal suit with black chinos and an open-necked grey silk shirt, which made him look younger and even sexier. 'Did you?' she asked vaguely, knowing only too well that he had.

'Come into the dining room,' he urged her. 'I was just about to eat, and you're obviously hungry. Where have you been all day? Mehrdad wanted to speak to you before he left, about the charity.'

'I went for a walk and took in a movie.'

'Then you weren't avoiding us all?'

'Why would I do that?' asked Chloe.

'That's what I asked myself. I couldn't think of any reason at all.' Although he sounded serious, his blue eyes were amused, and Chloe knew that he could read her like an open book.

For the first part of the meal, the talk was general. Carlos discussed the state of the economy, its effect on women's fashions, and football, while Chloe simply listened and occasionally responded while waiting for him to get to the point.

It wasn't until dessert that he finally made his move. 'So tell me, Chloe, what did you feel like when Livia's cream was massaged into you?' he asked casually.

Immediately Chloe recalled exactly how she'd felt; the way her nipples had swelled and her body had become desperate for sexual satisfaction. 'I can't remember,' she lied.

Carlos gave a short laugh. 'You mean you don't want to tell me! There's no point in being shy, Chloe, not after last night. Describe it to me. I want to hear you say it. It's all part of learning to discard your inhibitions, and a vital part of your time with me.'

Chloe shifted uneasily in her seat. 'I don't want to tell you.'

He sighed. 'That's precisely why you have to do it. Don't disappoint me now, not after doing so well last night.'

Pushing away her mango sorbet, Chloe folded her hands in her lap and stared down at the polished mahogany table top. 'It made me feel hot,' she explained softly. 'It was as though my body was burning.'

He stared at her, his eyes bright with eager anticipation. 'And how did that make you feel?'

'I don't know what you mean.'

'Yes you do, now tell me.'

She did know, but somehow thinking back over it, and realising how she must have looked to the watching Carlos, was almost worse than having it happen to her. 'It made me want sex,' she whispered.

'I know that. I want you to describe the way your breasts felt, in fact how every part of your body felt. Describe it all, leave nothing out.'

'My skin felt too tight for my body,' murmured Chloe, her cheeks going red with embarrassment. 'It was as though I was swelling up inside it, and my breasts were hot and throbbing. All my body seemed to be pulsating. I ached deep inside, and I didn't think that I'd ever be able to be satisfied, no matter—' She broke off as the maid came in to clear the table.

'Carry on,' said Carlos sternly, signalling for the maid to remain in the room.

Chloe wanted to disappear through the floor, but she knew that this was all part of the discipline, and she was determined not to fail now. 'No matter how many orgasms I had,' she said clearly.

Freed by a brief hand signal from her employer, the maid hurried away. Carlos smiled down the table at Chloe. 'You see, it wasn't so difficult after all, was it?'

'Yes, it was.'

'Didn't you enjoy telling me? Not even a little bit?'

'No,' said Chloe firmly, but she had. As she'd been talking she'd known that Carlos was becoming excited by her words, and this had made her feel powerful and sexy.

'You wanted me last night, didn't you?' continued Carlos.

'I . . .'

'When I took you back to your bedroom, you wanted me to stay.'

'Perhaps I did.'

He got to his feet, then walked swiftly round to where she was sitting and put his hands on her shoulders, his fingers massaging her muscles with slow, rhythmic strokes. 'I want you now,' he murmured, bending down so that his mouth was against her ear. She shivered, feeling his breath against her skin. 'Now,' he repeated, catching hold of her by her wrist and pulling her out of her chair.

Before she knew what was happening, she was pinned against the wall, and his hands were pushing her skirt up round her waist as he deftly unfastened his chinos. He was moving himself against her all the time, his hips grinding into hers, and when she felt him pulling her panties to one side her excitement grew.

As he rested the swollen head of his erection against her, she felt her sex lips opening up for him, and very quickly he was rubbing himself against her clitoris until she was whimpering with excitement.

'I wanted to do this last night,' he groaned, and then he thrust fiercely into her, his hands gripping her hips so that he could rock her lower body back and forth as he moved steadily in and out of her.

He was breathing rapidly, and when his mouth covered hers and his tongue began to invade her mouth, Chloe's body rushed towards a climax. She moaned against his mouth as the hot, liquid pleasure flooded through her, and then her muscles were contracting tightly around him and within seconds he was spasming inside her, his whole body juddering with the intensity of his climax.

When his hands released her, Chloe slumped against the wall, wishing that she could just slide down it and sink on to the floor. Her legs felt weak and her whole body was soft and relaxed. It had been such a swift and yet personal coupling that for the first time she felt close to the Brazilian who was both her lover and her tutor.

After he'd released her, Carlos looked at her with a fleeting expression of surprise on his face, but then he turned away. 'It's a pity Mehrdad wasn't here to see that. He'd have enjoyed it,' he remarked, sitting down in his chair again. 'I think we'll have coffee in the drawing room now, Chloe. We can discuss the charity dinner while we drink it.'

Sitting in one of the large armchairs in the drawing room, Carlos studied Chloe as she perched on the edge of the sofa, her knees together and her hands in her lap like a dutiful schoolgirl. It was a picture strangely at odds with how she'd looked the previous night, when she'd twisted and turned in the middle of the vast bed, her hair tousled and soaked with sweat as she'd reached peak after peak of pleasure while Livia, Mehrdad and Mike had played with her deliciously sensual body.

Even now, after taking her so swiftly in the dining room, Carlos still wanted her. He wanted to possess her body and soul, to turn her inside out, watching her force herself through every new sexual boundary that she met until finally she decided that she could no longer discipline her body in the way he wanted. Only then, when she failed, would he cease to want her.

'I need five more tickets for the top table at the dinner,' he explained. 'Mehrdad will be making a significant donation to the Street Children of Brazil fund tomorrow. He also wants to buy tickets for himself, Fiona, Chris and Natasha for the dinner, and we'd better have a ticket for Mike, otherwise the numbers will be wrong.'

Chloe frowned. 'No they won't. You and Livia plus Mehrdad, Fiona, Chris and Natasha is fine. It's Mike who makes the numbers wrong.'

'You forget that you're coming with us,' he reminded her gently, knowing full well that she hadn't forgotten.

'I'm going to be sitting at the top table, but I'm not there with you,' she explained carefully.

'You'll be alone?'

'Of course. It doesn't bother me. I'm only at the top table because you want me there. It's made things quite awkward with some of the other girls.'

'That's interesting. Why does it affect anyone else?'

'They don't think I should be with the VIPs. I'm only a very junior assistant; there are a lot of other people working there who are far more entitled to sit at the top table than I am.'

'But they wouldn't interest me,' he said with a laugh.

'I can hardly tell them that!' retorted Chloe. 'Now you're saying that if I'm with your party, we need Mike as well, but I don't want a partner. I shall have lots of things to do that evening.'

Carlos shook his head. 'I don't think so, Chloe. I want you by my side, sitting on my right hand, in fact. I also want Livia sitting next to your chairman, Sir Lionel. She should give him an interesting evening and I shall enjoy watching her seduce him with her charms.'

'But his wife will be there!'

'Precisely. As for you, I shall be choosing your dress for the evening, and I don't want you wearing any underwear. Is that clear?'

Chloe shook her head. 'I'm sorry, Carlos, but I can't do that. I'll be sacked if I step out of line at the dinner, and the job means a lot to me.'

He was faintly touched by her anxiety, but it also increased his excitement. 'Nothing will happen to endanger your job, I promise you. Only you and I will know what happens to you at the dinner.'

'I can't do it, Carlos, and I don't think I can sit Livia next to Sir Lionel either. It wouldn't be right.'

Carlos was pleased she was resisting him. There would be no fun in teaching her his kind of discipline if she didn't kick against it. Most of the pleasure would come from forcing her to go against her natural instincts. That was why he was growing tired of Livia; she would probably have chosen to do most of the things he made her do anyway.

'There's no choice,' he said quietly. 'I'm ordering you to do this, Chloe. You have to obey my rules, just as you used to obey the rules of your religious order, remember?'

'But I thought that was only here, inside this house,' exclaimed Chloe.

'You know better than that. Remember the pub at Richmond?'

'That was different. It wasn't with people I knew, people I had to work with every day.'

'Of course not, because it was in your early days. You were a sexual novice then, but after last night that term hardly applies to you any more. Be honest, doesn't the idea of sitting next to me half-naked and aroused, without knowing what's going to happen to you, intrigue you?'

'I don't know how I'm going to get through the night,' she muttered, hanging her head.

'I notice you're no longer refusing.'

When Chloe didn't reply, he got up and went over to her. 'Arrange it all,' he commanded her, running his fingers through her hair and massaging her scalp lightly with his fingertips. As she gave a small sigh and moved her head back against his hand, he bent down, kissed the nape of her neck and then walked out of the room.

In his experience, combining firm authority with just a slight reminder of sensual pleasure was the best way to lead a reluctant but natural sensualist like Chloe further down the road of his choice.

He was amazed when Chloe ran after him, and caught up with him on the first-floor landing. 'What is it?' he asked sharply.

'It doesn't seem right that Mehrdad is giving the charity money because of last night.'

'Why not?'

'The things that we did were very private and personal. This makes it all seem like a business transaction.'

'Nonsense. You gave pleasure to Mehrdad and now he wants to thank you. I told him how much the charity meant to you and he sees it as a nice way of showing his gratitude.'

'I see,' she said thoughtfully, and for a fleeting moment he wondered exactly what she was thinking. 'Are there more tests for me to undergo after this?' she added.

He nodded. 'Naturally, several more.'

'And what happens if I pass them all?'

Carlos shrugged. 'I haven't thought that far ahead. What would you like to happen?'

She smiled sweetly at him. 'I haven't thought that far ahead either.'

Carlos was intrigued on two counts. First, no woman had ever said that to him before, and second, he had a feeling that she wasn't telling him the truth. That was good. Disciplining Chloe would be even more satisfying than he'd originally anticipated.

121

CHAPTER

14

When Chloe arrived at work the next morning, Lizzie was already at her desk. Glancing up at Chloe, she started to greet her, and then frowned. 'What's happened to you?' she asked.

'What do you mean?'

'Have you changed your hairstyle or something?'

'No.'

'Well you look different. New make-up?'

Chloe began to feel uncomfortable as Lizzie continued to study her. 'I'm two days older than when you last saw me, that's the only difference I can think of!'

'Something's happened,' declared Lizzie firmly. 'You've got a glow about you. I know; you're in love!'

'Of course I'm not in love. Heavens, is that list of phone calls for me? I'd better make a start on it.' With that she made her way past the still thoughtful-looking Lizzie and sat down at her own desk. 'By the way,' she added casually, 'Carlos would like some more tickets for the dinner next month.'

'Carlos?'

'Carlos Rocca.'

'I knew who you meant, I was just surprised to hear you calling him Carlos.'

'I *am* renting a room in his house, Lizzie. I can hardly call him Senhor Rocca all the time.'

'I'd have thought he was the kind of man who'd demand formality. Anyway, I'm afraid you'll have to tell your Carlos that the tickets are sold out. Sorry.'

'They can't be!'

'Why not? Thanks to some free advertising that Annabel managed to get out of a contact in the magazine world last week, the final few were snapped up late Friday night after you dashed off.'

'But Mehrdad—'

'Who?' asked Lizzie abruptly.

'He's one of Carlos's friends. His name's Mehrdad and he wanted to come to the dinner. I think Carlos virtually promised him a place at the top table.'

'Is that Mehrdad Kervani?'

'I've no idea. Why, do you know him?'

'I certainly do! He brought in a cheque for ten thousand pounds this morning, but he didn't ask for any tickets for the dinner.'

'That's probably because Carlos had said he'd get them for him,' explained Chloe.

'Well, for ten thousand pounds I think we can make the top table a little bit bigger, don't you?' said Lizzie with a laugh. 'You know, for an ex-nun who didn't know anyone in this country, you've made some very rich and useful contacts since you joined us. What's the secret of your success?'

'I don't know Mehrdad personally,' lied Chloe, trying not to remember the way he'd placed the vibrator deep inside her as her frantic flesh throbbed and longed for stimulation.

'Really? You know Carlos Rocca pretty personally though. Is this Mehrdad guy coming as his guest?'

'Yes, along with his wife, another couple and a male friend.'

Lizzie smiled. 'I see, a spare male. Would this be someone to keep you company?'

'No it would not!'

'Doesn't matter to me,' said Lizzie reassuringly. 'One word of advice though. I should keep a bit quiet about your closeness to our esteemed patron. Some of the other girls might read more into it than you claim exists. I suppose Senhor Rocca has very definite ideas about where he wants his new guests seated as well, has he?'

'Some,' admitted Chloe. 'He wants me to sit on his right and his partner Livia to sit next to Sir Lionel. Will that be possible?'

'I don't know what Sir Lionel will make of an exotic Brazilian beauty sitting next to him. She is beautiful, I take it?'

'Yes, very beautiful.'

'In that case, why does Senhor Rocca want you on his right and not his mistress?'

'No idea,' said Chloe abruptly. 'I'm going to do my phoning from the small back office. It's quieter there.'

It was obvious that Lizzie knew something strange was going on, but Chloe hoped that her own apparent naïvety would stop the other woman from guessing the bizarre and shaming truth.

As usual on a Monday there was a lot of work to do, and Chloe was able to keep out of Lizzie's way until the end of the day. Aware that the older woman was concerned, she was anxious not to get into any kind of deep conversation with her.

Usually Lizzie left promptly on a Monday night, to go to badminton, so Chloe waited until six o'clock to go into the main office and collect her things. However, Lizzie was still there.

'Where have you been hiding yourself all day?' she asked Chloe.

'I haven't been hiding, I've just been busy. You saw how many phone calls I had to make and—'

'Didn't you even take a lunch break?'

Chloe shook her head. 'Not today.'

Lizzie frowned. 'What's happening to you, Chloe?'

'Nothing's happening to me. It isn't a crime to be busy, is it?'

'I didn't mean that, and you know it. Why is Senhor Rocca so determined to have you sitting next to him at our charity dinner? And why did this Mehrdad man give us such a massive donation, when as far as I know he'd never had anything to do with us before?'

Chloe shrugged. 'I've no idea.'

'I don't think that's true. I didn't mention it earlier, but he said it was in memory of you. For one dreadful moment I thought you'd died over the weekend. I started to ask him what had happened, and he laughed. He actually laughed, as though I'd said something incredibly amusing. What was funny about me thinking you were dead? When people give money to charities in memory of another person it's usually because they've died. Since you clearly didn't die, what did you do to make him think so highly of you?'

Chloe's mind went completely blank. 'What do you think I did, Lizzie?' she asked at last.

'I have absolutely no idea.'

'Then why are you sounding so accusing?'

'Because he's a handsome, sophisticated man, and so is Carlos Rocca. They're men of the world, Chloe. They're intrigued by innocent young women like you, but they discard them when they get bored. I don't want you hurt. You don't have any family to advise you, and in a way I feel responsible for you. There is something going on, isn't there?'

'No, there isn't, but I understand what you're saying and

I'm not completely stupid. Believe me, there's nothing for you to worry about. I'm fine. I met Mehrdad over the weekend. He and his wife were staying with Carlos and Livia. I talked to Mehrdad about my time in Brazil. I explained how I'd come back to England feeling totally disillusioned, but that working for the charity here had proved very satisfying. He was interested, and I suppose he wanted to do something to help. Although ten thousand pounds is a lot to us, to a man like him it's nothing.'

'Rich people are usually less willing to part with their money than poorer ones,' said Lizzie drily. 'What was this memory he mentioned then?'

'I suppose he meant he remembered talking to me. I expect he expressed himself badly. His English isn't that good.'

Lizzie clearly didn't believe that. 'He's got an English wife, Chloe! I thought his English was excellent.'

'I don't know what you want me to say,' said Chloe. 'I've told you everything and—'

'Have you really, Chloe? Do you swear you've told me everything?'

Reluctantly Chloe looked Lizzie directly in the eye, and found herself unable to swear to a lie. 'Maybe not,' she conceded.

Lizzie sighed. 'I thought as much. I don't want any details, it's none of my business anyway, but please be careful, Chloe. You don't belong in the kind of world men like that inhabit. One day they'll move on and leave you behind. What will you do then?'

'It's not like that,' said Chloe soothingly. 'Honestly, Lizzie, I'm all right. I know what I'm doing. Besides, think what the charity can do with the money!'

'Bugger the charity,' said Lizzie sharply. 'I'm worried about you. I'd rather we had to hold an extra fifty raffles than think you were getting caught up in things you didn't understand, even if we got a million pounds as a result. I care about you, Chloe, and right now I'm very worried.'

Chloe was touched. She knew that Lizzie was telling her the truth, and was grateful for the older woman's concern, but it was far too late. She was already trapped in Carlos's world, addicted to the disciplined sexuality that he was teaching her.

Despite Livia's beauty and her independent wealth, Chloe had seen flashes of fear in the Brazilian girl's eyes over the weekend, fear that she was losing her lover. It was clear to Chloe that without Carlos Livia wouldn't know how to exist. She'd spent so long in his world of dark, decadent pleasure that she wouldn't be able to survive without it. Livia was a permanent warning to Chloe of the danger of total dependence on the handsome Brazilian, and a far more effective one than Lizzie's anxious words.

'You don't need to worry,' she said quietly. 'I'll be fine.'

'You're not the first girl to have said those words and realised too late that she was wrong.'

'Perhaps I'll be the first to say them and discover I was right! I must dash now. You've missed your badminton class, haven't you?'

Lizzie nodded. 'It doesn't matter. I had to talk to you. Now that I have, it's your decision, but at least I've warned you. From now on I won't mention anything about your private life again, okay?'

Chloe smiled. 'Is that a promise?'

'As long as you behave at the dinner, yes, it's a promise,' retorted Lizzie with a laugh.

Walking back to Carlos's house, Chloe thought about her friend's final words and shivered. She had a feeling that Carlos intended her to behave very badly at the dinner. She just had to hope that somehow she could disguise the fact from Lizzie, and all the other people from work who'd be there that night.

Taking out her key to the front door, her heart started to beat faster, and her mouth went dry. It was time for the discipline to begin again.

CHAPTER

15

'Here she comes,' said Carlos to Livia as he looked out of the drawing room window and saw Chloe walking towards the house.

Livia glanced sideways at him. 'You sound excited.'

'I am excited. This evening should be very interesting for both of us.'

'Both meaning you and Chloe?'

He nodded, untroubled by her obvious irritation. It was Chloe who interested him at the moment. She would find what he had planned for her this evening difficult, and watching her struggle would arouse him in a way that Livia no longer had the power to do.

Before Chloe had time to insert her key in the lock, Carlos opened the front door for her and saw a flicker of apprehension in her eyes, but an apprehension that was tinged with excitement.

'I've been waiting for you,' he said quietly. 'Today I read a book of English nursery rhymes. Do you know the one about Little Tommy Tucker?'

Chloe smiled. 'Of course I do. He had to sing for his supper.'

'Which is precisely what you will have to do tonight. Not

literally, of course, but the concept is the same. Before you can eat tonight, you must entertain me by showing me how disciplined your sexual responses have become.'

Chloe swallowed nervously. 'Straight away?'

'What's the point in waiting?'

'I need to shower and change.'

'Don't worry. I'll help you shower. Come upstairs now. Remember, obedience is necessary within any discipline. The nuns must have taught you that.'

Carlos could tell that Chloe, though clearly apprehensive, was also excited. Her eyes were bright, and there was a pink tinge to her cheeks. 'Follow me,' he said firmly, and without looking back he made his way up the stairs and into the bedroom that he and Livia shared.

'Leave the door open. Livia will be up in a moment. Take off your clothes and leave them on the floor. The shower is through here, in the bathroom.'

'I didn't know Livia was going to be with us,' murmured Chloe.

Carlos smiled to himself. He knew that everything would be more difficult for Chloe with Livia looking on and helping him. Obviously Chloe knew it too. That was good. It would add an edge of fear to everything she had to do, and fear could be a wonderful aphrodisiac.

Turning round, he saw her standing naked in the middle of the room. She looked very small and defenceless, and her almond-shaped grey eyes were enormous as she looked at him, waiting for her instructions. He had an almost overwhelming urge to take her there and then, but knew that he would only regret it. There would be time for that later, after she'd learnt to control her body's reactions. Her struggle would inflame him even more.

'Perhaps a bath, not a shower,' he mused aloud, and gestured for her to follow him into the en suite bathroom.

'Stand by the wall there while I fill the tub,' he said curtly, then turned on the taps so that the room quickly began to fill with steam.

Chloe watched Carlos bending over the bath and felt herself start to tremble. It was shaming, but already her body was hungry for him to begin arousing her. She was nervous as well, but that was only increasing her excitement, and she wondered what Lizzie would think if she could see her now.

When the bath was almost full, and the bubbles threatened to spill over on to the pale blue carpet, Carlos signalled for her to move over to his side. Then he straightened up and studied her naked body before running his hands down her sides, his fingers splaying out when he reached her waist. For a moment they danced over her leaping flesh, but then his hands moved on until he was caressing the calves of her legs and her ankles.

At another signal from him, Chloe stepped into the bath. As she lifted her right leg he rested his left hand on the inside of her thigh and brushed his fingertips against her dark pubic hair. Her breath caught in her throat, and immediately he removed his hand.

Once she was lying down in the water, he reached down into the foam and began to knead gently at her muscles. He started with her feet and worked his way upwards, finally concentrating on her shoulders and neck.

Her entire body seemed to become sexually alive beneath his caresses, and she couldn't stop herself from giving tiny sighs of pleasure as she revelled in the luxury of it all. He continued to massage her for a long time, until her eyes grew heavy and her lids began to droop. Then he stopped, and helped her out of the tub, before wrapping her in a thick, warm towel and proceeding to dry her. She couldn't remember when she'd last felt so relaxed.

When the towel was suddenly removed and she was once more naked, she felt bereft. 'That was wonderful,' she murmured.

'How nice,' said Livia coldly from the doorway, and hearing her voice brought Chloe out of the cocoon of sensual pleasure in which Carlos had so cunningly enveloped her.

'Recovered from your day at the office now?' he asked. Chloe nodded. She didn't want to speak, didn't want to do anything to break the spell sooner than was necessary. 'Good, then we can begin. Come back into the bedroom.'

Obediently she left the warm, steam-filled room and returned to the bedroom. The curtains had been shut against the early-evening sunlight, but the concealed lighting had been turned on and scented candles were burning in heavy iron candlesticks beside the bed. The heady smell of exotic spices filled Chloe's nostrils as she inhaled deeply.

Taking her by the hand, Carlos led her over to the bed and pushed her gently down until she was sitting near the bottom of it, while Livia stood watching her from the doorway into the bathroom. 'Move a little further back,' he said, and watched intently as she hitched herself up the soft duvet.

'That's excellent. I want you to masturbate yourself to orgasm for me, remembering to keep your clitoris exposed to my gaze all the time. After you've come once, I want you to make yourself come again as quickly as possible for a second time, with the same rule applying. Do you have any questions?'

'I don't know if I can do that,' cried Chloe. 'What if—'

'There are no what ifs here tonight, Chloe. Begin now, and remember, I shall know if you try to fake it.'

Chloe had no intention of trying to fake an orgasm, because she didn't know how to do it. Neither did she know if she'd be able to make herself come, not so coldly, without any help. However, as Carlos remained standing at the foot of the bed, his blue eyes hard and glittering with excitement, she felt her body start to respond to the challenge he'd set her.

Sliding her right hand down between her thighs, she lay back against the cushions in the middle of the bed, and then pulled her knees up towards her before letting them fall open so that she was totally exposed to Carlos's gaze.

She pressed the palm of her hand against herself, making sure that she was stimulating the top join of her outer sex lips. Slowly the first flickers of arousal began to dart through her lower belly, and she whimpered to herself as her sex lips started to part.

Glancing upwards, she saw that Carlos was breathing deeply, his tongue flicking over his lower lip to moisten it. She started to imagine what it would feel like to have his tongue where her fingers were, and immediately her juices began to flow.

Her sex was opening up rapidly now, and she withdrew her hand for a moment so that she could moisten her middle finger in her mouth. Then, when she let her hand snake down her body and between her outspread thighs again, it was easy for the damp finger to stroke the sides of her rapidly swelling clitoris.

Immediately she felt her abdominal muscles tighten, and her hips moved restlessly on the bed. The pressure began to build from deep inside her belly but then, as the sensations grew even more intense, her clitoris tried to retract beneath its protective hood.

133

'Push down,' demanded Carlos harshly. 'I told you to keep your clitoris visible to me at all times.'

Whimpering with the effort, Chloe did as she was told, and as her fingertip stroked the tip of the overstimulated bunch of nerve endings, the sensations overwhelmed her and a violent orgasm ripped through her body. With a sharp cry she felt her body spasm with ecstasy, and her legs trembled violently until the last delicious tendrils of pleasure died away.

'Again,' said Carlos firmly.

'Please, not yet!' cried Chloe, who knew how sensitive her clitoris would be at this moment.

'You have no choice. It's my wish, and you must obey my orders without question. That's what discipline is all about, remember?'

The fact that he and Livia were watching her, and that she was lying so utterly and shamelessly exposed should have made it impossible for Chloe to obey, but instead it had the opposite effect. Her treacherous body wanted to do as Carlos demanded, and craved the intense satisfaction of another climax.

Slowly, hesitantly, she moved her hand back between her thighs. This time she pressed against her pubic mound before moving her hand lower, and immediately tiny sparks started to run through her whole body. Without thinking, she began to massage her breasts with her left hand, and this increased her overall excitement.

By the time her fingers reached the hub of her sexuality, she was soaking wet there again, and the tip of her middle finger slid over the swollen flesh, making her entire body swell and grow hot.

Her clitoris was tight and hard, aching with need, but the moment she allowed herself to touch it, she felt it disappear from beneath her finger. She groaned aloud with a mixture of disappointment and fear at Carlos's reaction.

'That's the second time I've lost sight of it, Chloe,' he reminded her.

'I didn't mean it to happen, I swear I didn't,' she cried, trying desperately to push back the covering membrane.

'Livia, you'll have to assist,' said Carlos. 'Chloe will be punished later. First I want to see her make herself come for the second time.'

Within seconds the Brazilian girl was sitting next to Chloe. Her skilled fingers pushed at the offending skin until the throbbing, overstimulated clitoris was once more exposed. Aware of how sensitive it was, Chloe touched it very lightly on its side, but the resulting sensation was like a red-hot burning pain which lanced through her lower body, making her scream aloud.

'Continue,' ordered Carlos.

Chloe's body was in turmoil. The sensations were too intense, threatening to overwhelm her, and now she knew that when this was over she was going to be punished, yet still she continued to arouse her own throbbing flesh.

Gradually, as she adjusted to the painfully intense sensations she was causing herself, her body began to take perverse enjoyment in the sharp, searing flashes that were coursing through her. She could feel her stomach growing tight, and her breasts were throbbing, the nipples standing out rigidly from the surrounding flesh.

She needed to come, needed release from the terrible tension that was consuming her, and so she forced herself to stroke the cruelly exposed bunch of nerve endings one more time.

Immediately her body responded. All her muscles tightened yet further for one brief second, and then she was racked by another climax. She heard herself crying out incoherently as her body thrashed helplessly on the bed while Livia continued to prevent her clitoris from retreating beneath its protective hood.

Only when she was finally still, the sweat trickling between her breasts, did Carlos call Livia away from Chloe's side, and then the pair of them stood looking down at her as she shivered and gasped in the aftermath of her second orgasm.

'It seems that you still have difficulty in obeying my instructions,' remarked Carlos when she was finally still. 'I'm disappointed in you.'

'But really I tried!' she protested. 'It isn't something I've done before and—'

'Don't try and make excuses for yourself. I find it tedious in the extreme. Perhaps your punishment will help you to become more disciplined. Livia, fetch the footstool.'

Pushing herself up on one elbow, Chloe watched as the Brazilian girl placed a small padded footstool near the curtained window, just beneath one of the concealed lights. Then Carlos took hold of her hand, helping her off the huge bed before leading her over to the footstool. 'Stand on that,' he commanded her.

Chloe could feel her heart thudding against her ribs, and her breathing seemed constricted by fear. She didn't know what her punishment was going to be, but she was certain that it was going to test her in ways that she didn't even dare begin to imagine.

As soon as she'd stepped on to the low stool, Carlos pulled her hands roughly behind her back, and then she felt the touch of cold metal against her skin and heard a tiny click as handcuffs were fastened around her wrists. As a result, her shoulders were pulled back, and her breasts jutted out, caught in the beam from the concealed light.

Carlos ran the palm of his right hand over each of her

nipples in turn, then gave a low laugh as they quickly grew hard beneath his touch. 'Such eager little tips,' he murmured to himself. Chloe felt ashamed of her own response.

'Fetch the wooden box,' continued Carlos, and now Chloe's eyes turned to Livia, who opened one of the drawers in the dressing table and drew out a mahogany box with a lacquered lid. 'Stay where you are,' Carlos instructed Chloe as he opened the box and drew out a long ivory stick, thick at the base but tapering to a narrow point.

Next he poured some oil from a small glass phial into the palm of his left hand before rubbing this over the stick, which he then studied thoughtfully. 'Yes, that should be ideal, don't you think, Livia?'

'Perfect,' agreed his mistress with a smile.

Without saying another word, Carlos walked round behind Chloe. Then she felt him parting the cheeks of her bottom before, with a swift twisting movement, he inserted the ivory taper deep inside her rectum.

Chloe gave a gasp of protest, but he ignored her. 'Clench your muscles and keep it inside you,' he said curtly. 'If you let it fall out, I shall be very angry. This is your punishment, and I don't expect you to fail me again.'

Panic-stricken by the tone of his voice, Chloe quickly tightened her internal muscles, trying to get a grip on the slippery object, but it was difficult and she felt it start to slide out of her before finally managing to pull it back a little. In order to do as Carlos said, she had to keep her muscles tightly clenched and concentrate all the time.

Carlos nodded with satisfaction, and then patted her lightly on the bottom, an action that nearly made her release it by mistake. 'Excellent. Remember, no matter what I do to you, the ivory taper has to remain inside you.'

He was standing in front of her now, his strange blue eyes staring intently into her grey ones, but there was no flicker of sympathy on his face. Instead he looked both intrigued by her plight, and fiercely determined to teach her how to control herself in the way he wanted.

When he crouched down at her feet and ran his hands up the insides of her legs, she felt her heart sink. She knew that if he distracted her for even a moment, the taper would slip and she would have failed him yet again. 'Please don't touch me,' she whispered, but if he heard, he didn't acknowledge her words. His hands moved inexorably higher, and then he parted her sex lips and very gently inserted a finger inside her.

Her whole body jerked at this second invasion, and the taper slipped a fraction. Hastily she clenched the cheeks of her bottom, but then she felt Carlos's finger moving delicately around just inside the opening to her vagina, and her heart sank again. When he finally located her G-spot and started to press against it, the familiar hot, sweet pleasure began deep inside her belly and she grew frantic with fear.

'No! Don't do that to me, not now, please!' she begged him.

'Concentrate on the taper,' he murmured, as he continued to caress the sensitive nerve endings. Gritting her teeth, Chloe did as she was told. 'Good girl,' he said soothingly. 'Now grip my finger hard as well, but don't let the taper drop.'

In order to tighten her vaginal walls, Chloe had to move her belly inwards, and almost at once she felt the first contractions of an orgasm starting inside her. Crying out in protest, she struggled to quell the rising pressure but it was hopeless. Carlos's finger was stimulating her with the most cruelly delicate touch and that, combined with the heavy pressure of the ivory taper against the walls of her rectum, resulted in an uncontrollable climax that rushed upwards through her from her toes to the top of her head, in a moment of pure ecstasy.

When the blissful sensations finally died away, Chloe's muscles went limp, and before she had time to realise what was happening, the tapered ivory stick had slipped out and fallen to the carpet.

'The taper's out,' said Livia, satisfaction evident in her voice.

'I'm sorry,' whispered Chloe, but Carlos simply stared at her in silence. Then he grabbed her roughly by the arms, and propelled her across the room and on to the bed. He pushed her on to her back, and she winced as her wrists were trapped behind her.

However, she didn't have long to think about the discomfort in her wrists, because within seconds, Carlos was sitting astride the tops of her thighs and flicking at the tender skin of her stomach with the backs of his fingers.

The blows stung, her flesh grew hot; and then, when he began to flick at her rapidly hardening nipples in the same way, she felt the first treacherous tendrils of desire start to snake through the pit of her belly again.

'You want to come again, don't you?' demanded Carlos, who had been watching her closely.

'Yes,' she admitted, not daring to lie to him.

'Then you must do better this time, otherwise you won't get any satisfaction tonight. Do you understand?'

She could have wept with the frustration and humiliation of it all, and felt the tears welling up behind her eyes, but Carlos ignored them. He simply pulled her off the bed, bundled her back on to the footstool and inserted the ivory taper once more.

As soon as it was deep inside her, he called Livia over and she knelt at Chloe's feet. This time she was the one who opened her up, only where Carlos had used his finger,

Livia used her skilled tongue. She licked and nibbled at Chloe's frantic flesh, drawing her clitoris into her mouth and sucking lightly on it before letting her tongue sweep up and down the moist channel of flesh between her inner lips.

All the time Livia was working on her, Chloe could feel her body swelling, her nipples hardening and the hot pulse of an impending orgasm throbbing behind her clitoris. She tried desperately to divert herself from all the exquisite sensations that were building up in her. Frantically she concentrated on keeping the taper in place, on clenching her buttocks and ignoring all the other signals that her straining body was sending her.

When she felt her muscles drawing inwards in preparation for a climax, she deliberately made most of her body go limp, so that all her energy was directed at keeping the cruelly slippery taper inside her, and for a brief moment she thought that she'd truly learnt to discipline herself.

Livia, however, was determined not to let Chloe triumph. Realising that the other girl's orgasm was starting to recede, she opened her up even more and then lightly drew the pointed tip of her tongue across the opening of Chloe's urethra.

For Chloe, momentarily relaxed and off guard, the sudden streak of piercing pleasure that seared through her was fatal. With a cry of anguish she felt her tormented body begin to spasm with a sharply intense sensation that was almost too much for the already overstretched nerve endings to tolerate. Suddenly she felt herself coming in wave after wave of violent shudders that left her screaming in helpless despair.

'I'm sorry,' she cried as Livia moved away and Carlos stood in front of her once more, the taper in his hand.

'There's no need to be sorry. The taper only fell out at the very end. You've made excellent progress. I don't think you need it inside you again. I'll take its place.'

'But she failed!' cried Livia.

'She's only a novice. We have to make allowances. You can go now, Livia. This final part of the discipline is a private affair.'

As Livia slammed the bedroom door shut behind her, Carlos picked Chloe up and carried her over to the bed.

CHAPTER

16

A ware that the Brazilian girl had gone, Chloe relaxed a little. The discipline that Carlos was teaching her was always hard, but whenever Livia was around it seemed almost impossible for her to satisfy the two of them.

She lay on the bed, watching as Carlos quickly took off his clothes. His erection was rock hard, and he was breathing heavily as he approached her. Silently he knelt on the bed, with the lower half of his legs tucked beneath him, so that the backs of his thighs were resting against his calves.

Once he was comfortable, he reached for Chloe, turning her over as he manoeuvred her into position. Then he pulled her down against him, until she could feel the end of his straining cock nudging between her buttocks.

Realising what he intended to do, she made a small sound of protest. She wasn't sure that she wanted any further stimulation inside her rectum. The walls were so thin, the nerve endings so sensitive that she was afraid it would be more than she could stand.

'Relax,' whispered Carlos. 'You'll enjoy this, I promise you. Be good; you've done very well so far, don't spoil it for me now.'

Chloe wanted to please him, and wanted to be pleasured

herself, but it was impossible for her to relax completely. She felt Carlos's hands tighten on her hips, and then he pulled her body sharply downwards, and as she felt him thrusting deep inside her second opening, she gave an involuntary cry of fear.

He was so large inside her, filling her to capacity, and she began to move around, trying to ease the uncomfortable sensation of fullness. It worked, because as she moved, so the discomfort lessened, and instead darts of pleasure streaked through her. At the same time, Carlos reached round her and with his left hand began to massage her aching breasts, while his right hand moved between her thighs.

Her body jerked as his fingers located her slippery clitoris and he began to stroke the surrounding flesh until she was squirming with delight. He tightened his grip on her left breast, pulling on the nipple and pinching it hard before slowly releasing it.

A stab of pain streaked through her breast, but quickly died away as he then gently stroked the throbbing bud, and all the time his fingers were busy working between her thighs, teasing the swollen flesh with delicate, feather-light touches that made her clitoris grow hard and tight.

Both of them were breathing rapidly now, their excitement rising. She felt Carlos's tongue inside her ear and then he began to kiss the left side of her neck, occasionally biting at the tender flesh before licking at the abused spot with the tip of his tongue.

Chloe was almost out of her mind with excitement. She could feel him growing even harder inside her back passage, and every time her body twisted and turned with delight his penis rubbed against the thin walls of her rectum, driving her into a frenzy of pleasure.

'I want you to come now,' he whispered, his breath warm against her ear.

143

Chloe wanted to come as well. Her body was so tight that she felt she'd explode if she didn't, but despite everything that he was doing to her, she remained balanced on the edge of her climax.

'Hurry,' he urged her, his hips starting to move.

'I can't come!' she cried. 'It's so near, but . . .'

Before she could finish explaining, Carlos had gripped her clitoris between his finger and thumb and began to squeeze it, gently at first but then with increasing pressure. The first fleeting seconds of rising pleasure quickly vanished, and Chloe started to squirm as they were replaced by a soft ache that swiftly mounted to an almost unbearably intense pain.

'No!' she shouted, as the pain spread through her belly and thighs, but still he continued to squeeze remorselessly on the tiny little bunch of nerve endings. He was still massaging her left breast, and thrusting gently inside her rectum, but all she was aware of was the red-hot pain lancing through the very centre of her being.

Tears began to fill her eyes, but just at the moment that she started to sob, the sensation changed. The dark, painful heat became pleasurable, something that her body needed, craved for, and although she did cry, it was with delight.

Carlos seemed to have reduced her to nothing more than a bunch of frantic nerve endings, all clamouring for satisfaction. Her body was rigid with sexual tension, every muscle tight and aching, every sinew stretched to breaking point as she hovered for a moment, poised at the point of no return.

It didn't seem possible, but as her overstimulated body prepared for the moment of release, Carlos forced himself even deeper inside her, and she screamed with ecstasy as an incredible mixture of pain and pleasure flooded through her. Immediately she began to spasm in helpless convulsions, while Carlos moved rhythmically in and out of her.

As she wept and sobbed in a frenzy of emotion, twisting and turning uncontrollably, she felt his whole body tense. Gripping her breast even harder, he groaned with pleasure. Without thinking, Chloe tightened her sphincter muscles around his pulsating cock. She heard him gasp, and then he began to drive in and out of her even more fiercely, his arms almost crushing her body as he pulled her back against him, groaning loudly.

Finally his hips jerked rapidly, and as he came, Carlos bit on the lobe of Chloe's ear in an animal-like frenzy of passion. When he relaxed, Chloe slumped back against him. She was aware that while this dark, pain-filled pleasure had been something entirely new for her, Carlos had been highly aroused by her reactions. This knowledge made her realise that even when she seemed totally under his control, she had power over him as well.

Lying in a tangled heap in the middle of the bed with Chloe, Carlos was surprised at how much he'd enjoyed their love-making. She'd accepted everything that he'd done almost without question, and he'd found her responses highly erotic. His resulting climax had been unusually intense, making him anxious to push her yet further in order to gain even more pleasure from her inherent sensuality.

Her eyes were closed, and he studied her with interest. She still looked extremely young and innocent, not very different to how she'd looked when he'd first seen her as a novice nun in Brazil. She was different, of course, but so far he didn't feel that he'd touched her soul, and he wanted to. He wanted to take her into the world where he lived, and corrupt her totally. He needed to see her struggle still more against the discipline he insisted on, and watch the confusion in her eyes as her body betrayed her. Before he met her, he'd been feeling jaded, but now he was refreshed, and there was still so much for her to learn.

'Wake up,' he said sharply, determined that she should never know how close she sometimes came to touching him emotionally as well as physically.

Chloe's eyes flew open with gratifying speed. 'Did I fall asleep?' she asked anxiously.

'For a few seconds. I want to talk to you about a couple of things. First, the charity dinner. Did you get the extra tickets we need?'

It was hard for her to focus on such mundane matters. 'Yes, but it was difficult. They were all sold. Luckily—'

'I don't need the details. You definitely have all the tickets?'

Chloe nodded. 'Good. You enjoyed tonight, didn't you?'

Chloe hesitated. 'Some of it,' she admitted at last.

'All of it,' he said with a laugh. 'It took you a little time, but that was to be expected. No, I think this kind of pleasuring suits you. Perhaps you should wear an anal plug on the night of the charity dinner. It will keep you aroused, so that you're ready to climax whenever I want you to.'

He saw her eyes widen as she took in the implications of what he was saying. 'I can't have orgasms at the dinner,' she protested. 'We'll be at the top table, and besides—'

'You'll do whatever I want you to do on the night. This isn't only a social occasion, Chloe. It's another part of the discipline. That's why I wanted you at my table, and why I need Mehrdad and Mike there. You respond quickly to them. It should be an interesting evening.'

'If you say so,' she murmured, lowering her head so that he couldn't see the expression in her eyes. He nodded to himself. She would do whatever he ordered her to do, he was sure of it.

'Your next test comes before that, though,' he continued. 'When I made you masturbate yourself tonight, it was to prepare you for the weekend.'

Chloe looked up sharply, and her expression was wary. 'What do you mean?'

'You, Livia and I are going to Mehrdad and Fiona's garden party. He always holds a summer party for charity. This year he's decided to give the proceeds to yours. Isn't that good news?'

'I suppose so,' she conceded.

'He raises a lot of money, around twenty thousand pounds usually.'

'That much?'

'Yes, that much, which will make it all worth your while, I'm sure.'

'What do you mean?'

'I mean that you will be the main attraction. People will come and watch you pleasuring yourself in the marquee. Later, after you've had a rest, and providing you've performed satisfactorily, some of the more privileged guests will have their own chance to pleasure you. No doubt Mehrdad will lay down some ground rules, and work out how to decide the winner, but it should be interesting, don't you think?'

Chloe pulled herself upright, drawing away from him as she tried to clarify her thoughts, and he was amused by her need to physically distance herself from him in order to think coherently. It was a very satisfactory measure of the power that he now had over her mind.

'I'm not going to do that,' she said firmly, looking him directly in the eye as she spoke. 'By tying it in with the charity you're trying to make me feel guilty if I refuse, but I can't do it just for money.'

'It isn't money for you,' he said patiently. 'I could

understand your reluctance if it were, but it's for a good cause.'

'I think the fundraising committee would probably rather not have it,' she retorted.

'I don't suppose for one moment that they would care how it was raised. In any case, it's irrelevant. The money can go to another charity if that would make you happier. I wish you to go to the garden party and be the afternoon's entertainment. Learning to lose your inhibitions in front of strangers is part of the discipline. All Mehrdad's friends are like-minded. No one will be shocked.'

'I can't do it. I'm sorry, Carlos, but it's impossible.'

Reaching out, he stroked the side of her face in a gentle caress. 'You can do anything you choose, you know that.'

She looked close to tears again. 'I can't do this, I really can't. I'm sorry, but you're asking too much of me.'

'I'm not asking you,' said Carlos slowly, 'I'm ordering you.'

Chloe shook her head. 'It doesn't make any difference how you say it, I'm not going to do it, Carlos, and that's the end of it.'

He allowed himself to give a small sigh of apparent disappointment. 'In that case, Livia will take your place. Luckily, she understands the way the discipline works. Even now, after all this time with me, she would never dream of refusing such an instruction. I thought that you were a quick learner, but it seems I was wrong.'

'Perhaps later on, when I'm more relaxed with people I don't know,' murmured Chloe.

'There will be no "later on",' snapped Carlos.

'What do you mean?'

'I mean that the experiment is over. You had better start looking for somewhere else to live. It's time for us to part company.'

'But I don't want to leave!' wailed Chloe. Carlos felt a thrill of satisfaction run through him, which he was careful to conceal.

'You have no choice. It's a pity, because I think that your body has enjoyed much that we've done, but there it is. Perhaps you will meet someone else who can satisfy these new needs that I've aroused in you. I hope that's the case.'

Chloe's eyes were bright with anger now. 'No you don't. You hope that I spend the rest of my life searching for someone who can give me the same kind of feelings that you do.'

'It seems you have a very poor opinion of my character!'

'Don't laugh at me,' she continued furiously. 'You know perfectly well that I have to stay with you, that I need to go on with the discipline. How could I leave now? Especially after tonight.'

'That's your problem, not mine.'

For a moment, Carlos still wasn't certain that he'd judged the moment right, that she was going to give in, but then, as her shoulders slumped, he relaxed. He'd been right. She was addicted to his ways, desperate to learn more, and for this reason, if no other, she'd agree.

'If I do it,' she said slowly, 'no one will know, will they?'

'Of course people will know. There will be a lot of guests and—'

'I meant no one except Mehrdad's friends.'

'Of course not. He isn't planning on TV coverage. I doubt if your contribution could be broadcast even if he were!'

'I just don't want people at work to know,' she explained. 'How could I face them again if they knew the kind of things that you make me do?'

'I don't make you do anything, Chloe,' he reminded her. 'You choose to do these things, because they give you pleasure. As for people at work finding out, how could they?'

'They don't all give me pleasure,' she muttered.

Carlos quickly tweaked her left nipple, which was still red from where he'd been pinching it earlier. It immediately grew hard, and he laughed. 'In the end, it all gives you pleasure. There's no point in denying it. Why be ashamed?'

'I can't help it. I feel as though it's wrong. Normal people don't do the things that you do to me.'

'How do you know? And what is a normal person anyway? Answer me that, Chloe. Can I tell Mehrdad that you're willing to entertain his guests as I promised?'

Chloe nodded.

'I want to hear you say it,' insisted Carlos.

'Yes,' she whispered, and the fact that she was clearly ashamed re-aroused Carlos, who felt himself start to harden again.

'You'd better get dressed and go down to dinner,' he said abruptly. 'I'm eating out with Mehrdad tonight. I'll give him the good news then. Now please return to your own room.'

He saw how confused she was by his sudden change of mood, but that didn't matter. It would keep her on edge, and in any case it was far better that she was confused than realise quite how powerfully she was beginning to affect him.

CHAPTER

17

By Thursday, all that Chloe could think about was Mehrdad's garden party. As each day passed, it drew inexorably nearer, and her dreams were filled with frightening yet arousing sexual images that made her wake up sweating with fear, although the details were infuriatingly elusive.

'You're late,' said Lizzie the moment Chloe walked into the office.

'Sorry, I overslept.'

Lizzie glanced at her. 'You still look tired.'

'I'm not sleeping well at the moment.'

'I hope you can lay your hands on all the lists I gave you to type up for the dinner; the names of people coming, the seating plan, menu, arrangements for flowers and so on.'

'Of course I can.'

'Good, then you can keep me company when the hotel's restaurant manager arrives this morning. I've lost track of all that information, too many other things to do, I'm afraid. You don't mind sitting in on the meeting with me, do you?'

Chloe was pleased that she'd have something to distract her from the prospect of Saturday. 'I'd like that,' she said with perfect honesty.

'In that case, would you collect him from the front office and take him through into the small back room? I'll be with you in about five minutes. Offer him coffee or something while you're waiting.'

Out in the front office, a tall young man in his early thirties was standing waiting. He had short dark-brown hair, a pale complexion and very dark eyes. When Chloe walked towards him he smiled at her, and she noticed that his mouth was full and sensual. He looked more like a classical actor than a restaurant manager, and for a brief moment she pictured him naked, lying next to her in the middle of Carlos's bed.

Horrified by her wanton thoughts, she put on her most businesslike expression and held out her hand in greeting. 'Hi, I'm Chloe Reynolds, Lizzie's assistant. Sorry we've kept you waiting. If you'd like to come through into the back room, I'll get you a coffee. Lizzie won't be five minutes.'

He smiled at her and his handshake was firm. 'Hi, I'm Rob. Don't worry about it. Today's my day off, there's no rush.'

'You have to work on your day off?' asked Chloe, leading him into the tiny room that immediately he seemed to fill.

'Not usually, but I was told this was going to take quite some time. As it's for charity, I want to make sure my team get everything right, so I thought I'd come when time didn't matter. When I'm working, I'm looking at my watch every five minutes.'

'You mean your team doesn't always get everything right?' asked Chloe teasingly.

'Not always,' he said with a wry smile. 'We try, but it's amazing how many things can go wrong in a restaurant, however carefully you plan every detail. Don't worry, if anything should go wrong, you can ask for a large refund, but don't tell the hotel management that I suggested it!'

'I won't. By the way, the coffee's awful,' she added, handing him a mug.

He took a sip and grimaced. 'You're not kidding!'

'Sorry,' apologised Chloe.

'You've nothing to be sorry about,' said Rob, looking at her admiringly.

Chloe felt herself starting to respond to his admiration. He was very good-looking, and the expression in his dark eyes suggested to her that there was probably more to him than met the eye. To her embarrassment she felt her nipples growing hard, and felt certain he must know what was happening.

'Hi, guys!' said Lizzie, breezing into the room and shattering the atmosphere. 'Okay, I'm here now, so let's get down to it. Chloe, you'd better introduce me to this handsome young man.'

Within half an hour, Lizzie was busy flirting with Rob as the two of them talked about the arrangements, and finally Chloe decided to leave. 'Do you still need me?' she asked. Lizzie shook her head, and carried on chatting in an animated fashion with Rob, so Chloe returned to her office.

She didn't see Rob go, but for the rest of the day she had to listen to Lizzie enthusing about the young man's charm, good looks and apparent fervent interest in their charity. Deciding that he was the kind of man who made every woman feel special, Chloe put Rob out of her mind. She certainly didn't need any more complications in her life at the moment; the forthcoming weekend was more than enough for her.

It was six-thirty before she left work. Feeling restless, she decided to go to the nearest wine bar and have a drink before returning to Carlos's house. She found a quiet table in a corner of the room, and sat there nursing her glass of Pinot Grigio and trying to calm her mind.

'Hello again,' said a familiar voice, suddenly interrupting her reverie. 'Do you mind if I join you?'

'Rob, how nice! I didn't see you come in.'

'I was already here,' he explained. 'I hoped I'd see you again before the dinner. How long have you been working for Lizzie?' Chloe opened her mouth to reply, but at that moment he touched her gently on the wrist. 'Let me get you another glass of wine first.'

'I've hardly started this one!'

'It will save me getting up once we're chatting.'

Chloe watched him make his way to the bar. He was well over six feet tall, with broad shoulders and slender hips. She noticed that most of the other women in the wine bar were watching him too, but he seemed unaware of their interest.

Once he returned to their table, the pair of them started to talk about their jobs. All the time they were talking, Rob kept touching her lightly on the arm, his gaze never leaving her. She wondered if he had some kind of sixth sense that was telling him her sexual secrets, because she couldn't think of any other reason why he'd be quite so interested.

As they laughed, talked and flirted mildly, Chloe suddenly knew that she wanted him. She was tired of always being told who she was to sleep with, and how she had to do it. She wanted Rob, and on her own terms. Leaning forward, she cut straight through what he was saying. 'It's stuffy in here,' she murmured. 'Why don't we drive out of London and go for a walk somewhere?'

Rob stopped what he was saying in mid-sentence and stared at her. For a dreadful moment, Chloe thought that she'd misjudged him, and that his interest in her wasn't sexual at all. Although shaken by her own behaviour, she managed to keep looking directly at him, and saw his eyes darken with desire and excitement.

'Good idea,' he said hastily, and without even finishing their drinks they hurried outside.

Luckily his car was parked nearby, and soon they were driving through London, only suddenly there was no conversation between them. Chloe was reminded of her drive with Mike, and this increased her sexual excitement.

'Have you any ideas about where we could go?' she asked.

'I thought Richmond Park. It's a nice place to walk, very relaxing.' She could hear the irony in his voice, and felt relieved. Clearly he understood what she wanted of him, and was anxious to respond. 'Do you have a partner?' he continued.

'No, before I came back to London a few weeks ago, I was living in Brazil, training to be a nun,' she explained.

'A nun? You're joking!'

'I'm not joking. I was very upset when I left. It was something I'd always wanted to do.'

Rob glanced sideways at her. 'Why?'

'Because I was attracted by their disciplined way of life.'

'Really? I can't imagine anything worse myself. I take it you're not, well, you know . . .' He tailed off awkwardly.

'No, I'm not at all like a nun now,' Chloe assured him.

Rob laughed. 'I didn't think you were. It was a bit of a shock hearing you say it, that's all. It's a turn-on though.'

'Is it?'

'Of course it is. At first I thought that was why you were saying it, but it's true, isn't it? You really were a nun once?'

'A novice nun,' she explained, and he rested his left hand on her knee for a moment, his fingers stroking her bare skin. She shivered. 'Are we nearly there?'

'Yes, I turn off here. We'll have to hurry. Once it starts to get dark they lock the gates.'

Hastily he parked the car and then, hand in hand, they

began to walk along the footpath that led towards the trees and dense bushes on the far side of the park. As they walked, his thumb stroked the sensitive skin on the inside of her wrist and she felt herself start to tremble with excitement.

It was a warm summer's evening, and there were a lot of people in the park. Looking around, Rob made a sound of irritation. 'Doesn't look as though we'll be able to get any privacy,' he muttered.

'Don't worry about it,' replied Chloe, trying not to sound too disappointed, but even as she spoke her mind was racing as she tried to work out what they could do. She wanted Rob urgently, tonight, and for once she was going to have what she wanted.

Soon they reached an area of ferns and bushes that was a little off the beaten track. Quickly she pulled on Rob's arm, taking him so much by surprise that he nearly fell. With a laugh, Chloe plunged deeper into the ferns and then lay down, dragging him down after her.

Once they were on the ground, the lush ferns closed over their heads, and they were lost in their own world. Quickly, without giving Rob time to make a move, Chloe unfastened the top buttons of her blouse and removed her panties, then rolled on top of Rob, so that she was crouching astride his thighs.

With an excited moan, Rob reached up and pushed her bra up over her breasts, so that he could fondle her nipples. The moment his hands touched her excited flesh, Chloe began to moan with delight, wriggling around frantically on Rob so that her aching clitoris could be stimulated.

Releasing her breasts, Rob fumbled with his trousers, but Chloe slapped his hands away. This time she was going to stay in control. Quickly she unzipped his flies and then slid a hand inside the opening of his boxer shorts until his swollen purple-headed cock sprang free.

Putting her hands on each side of his head, she leant forward, raising her hips up and then slowly lowering herself on to him, while Rob continued to play with her breasts, straining to draw a nipple into his mouth.

He sighed as the velvet tip of his erection slid inside her, but Chloe only tightened around him for a brief moment before raising herself off him again. 'What are you doing?' he asked, trying to pull her back down on top of him.

'Stop talking, leave it all to me,' she said sharply. For a moment his eyes were puzzled, but then he obeyed her, and she saw that his erection had grown even harder. Carefully she lowered herself on to him once more, and this time she contracted her internal muscles around him several times, until she felt the first tingles of an impending climax start to spread through her.

As soon as that happened, she raised herself off him again, and when he made a sound of protest, she flicked at his straining cock with her fingers, giving him a light but stinging blow.

'Ouch!' yelped Rob, and Chloe quickly put a hand over his mouth as she heard the voices of people on the path close by. For several seconds the two of them remained in frozen silence, hardly daring to breathe, but as the voices died away, Rob reached desperately for Chloe's hips.

'Don't touch me,' she warned him. 'If you do, I shall get up and go.'

'For God's sake, stop tormenting me like this,' he muttered.

With a soft laugh, Chloe sank down on him for a third time, but it was all too much for Rob. Grabbing hold of her hips, he flipped her over on to her back, while remaining firmly inside her, and then began to move rhythmically in and out of her, sliding up and down her sweat-soaked body.

Chloe was close to coming now; she could feel the wonderful hot warmth waiting to flood through her, but she knew that her aching clitoris needed to be touched before she could climax.

'Touch me there,' she begged Rob, moving her hips to show him what she meant.

'You're meant to be in charge, you do it,' he gasped, his own climax clearly very near.

Quickly Chloe slid her hand down between their bodies, and when her fingers caressed the side of the stem of the swollen little nub, her whole body jerked as an electric current seemed to streak through her.

Rob was still thrusting deeply into her, while his hands squeezed her breasts and his fingers teased her straining nipples. Lightly, delicately, she allowed her fingers to continue stroking her frantic clitoris. Within seconds she felt the muscles behind her pubic mound gathering together, and then her orgasm rushed through her in a hot, liquid flood of ecstasy.

As her body spasmed, she tightened around Rob and with a loud cry of triumph he came too, shuddering violently as his hands gripped her aching breasts convulsively.

Only when both their bodies were finally still did Chloe become aware of the broken ferns beneath her back, and the sounds of people walking near by. Breathing heavily, she stared up at Rob, and he gazed back at her in approval. 'I think you were right to leave the nunnery,' he said at last as he rolled off her.

'So do I,' agreed Chloe, realising that one of the buttons on the front of her blouse had come off during her rush to get partially undressed. 'This kind of behaviour would definitely have been frowned upon!'

At that moment, they heard a voice over a loud hailer warning them that the park gates would be closed in fifteen minutes. Laughing, they got to their feet and started to brush each other down, removing bits of fern and dead leaves from their clothes.

'That was incredible,' said Rob. 'When can I see you again?'

His question brought Chloe rapidly back down to earth. 'I don't know,' she muttered, remembering the forthcoming garden party.

'What do you mean? Didn't you enjoy it too? I thought you did; it certainly sounded as though—'

'I'm sorry,' said Chloe quickly. 'It isn't anything to do with you. I wasn't completely honest with you earlier.'

Rob's eyes darkened. 'In what way?'

'There's this man I'm seeing . . .'

'You said there wasn't anyone, that you used to be a nun.'

'I was a nun, and my relationship with this man is, well, complicated. He isn't exactly a boyfriend, but I'm not sure where the whole thing's leading.'

'I suppose he's married.' Rob was clearly very annoyed, and Chloe couldn't blame him. She'd got so carried away that she'd forgotten all about Carlos, and his hold over her.

There was no need for her to stay with Carlos, no need for her to go to Mehrdad's party, but she knew with absolute certainty that this was what she wanted to do.

'No, he isn't married, Rob. Look, I'm sorry, but I can't see you again until I've sorted out this other relationship.'

Rob shrugged. 'I can't complain. We only met today. The sex was great, and you never made me any promises. It's just that I thought we were good together.'

'We were, and we are,' said Chloe. 'Please, Rob, give me your phone number and then I can call you when I've got my life in order.'

'You aren't going to call, are you?' he said quietly. 'Be

159

honest with me, Chloe, I'd like to know. What did I do wrong?'

'Nothing,' Chloe assured him. 'It was great, the whole evening has been fantastic, but I'm not free at the moment. I will call you, really I will. I want to see you again, but it just isn't possible right now.'

They were soon back at the car, and when she got into the passenger seat, Rob scribbled on one of his company cards and then handed it to her. 'Here you are. I'll be waiting for your call, however long it takes.'

'Will you really?'

Rob nodded. 'Yes. My work involves long, unsociable hours. I don't want to get tied down at the moment, so I'll be around. Just ring when you're free.'

'Do you mean that literally, or figuratively?' queried Chloe.

Rob frowned. 'Mean what?'

'That you don't want to be tied down.'

He hesitated for a moment, and then smiled. 'I meant it figuratively. Literally, well, it might be fun to try.'

Neither of them said any more on the drive back into London, but when Chloe got Rob to let her out of the car a short distance from Carlos's house, he leant over and kissed her passionately on the mouth. 'That was a hell of an evening. I won't forget you for a long, long time, Chloe. Thanks.'

'I'll be in touch if I'm ever free,' she promised him, and then she reached over and ran her fingers up and down the quickly swelling bulge in his trousers before sliding out of the car. She meant it. She'd thoroughly enjoyed herself with Rob, and knew that she'd enjoy dominating him as well. The whole evening had made her realise that she wasn't totally dependent upon Carlos for sexual satisfaction.

However, good as it had been tonight, she hadn't had

the same feelings as she got when she was struggling to obey Carlos's demands. It hadn't been as intense or arousing, and she knew that it wasn't going to be easy to break away from him even if she wanted to.

After letting herself into the house, she went straight upstairs to change, and met Carlos on his way down. He eyed her thoughtfully, obviously taking in her dishevelled clothing and untidy hair.

'Al fresco sex tonight, Chloe? That's good. It should stand you in good stead for Saturday afternoon.' Immediately, all thoughts of her encounter with Rob were driven from her mind, and replaced by images of what lay ahead in Mehrdad's marquee.

CHAPTER

18

Friday went by far too quickly for Chloe's liking. Every hour that passed brought her closer to the garden party, and increased her fear.

The trouble was, it wasn't only fear. If that had been the case, she could have told Livia she could take her place, and then walked out of Carlos's life for ever. Unfortunately, the fact that she was also excited, and in a strange way looking forward to the event, meant this was impossible. It also increased her shame.

In order to distract herself, in her mind she replayed the sex that she and Rob had enjoyed the previous night. That cheered her, but did nothing to lessen the shame, because the old Chloe, the one who had walked so innocently into Carlos's home in Brazil, would never have behaved like that. She was rapidly becoming a stranger to herself.

By four thirty she was finding it impossible to concentrate on her work. Sighing, she pushed all the paperwork into her drawer and started to clear her desk.

'Finished?' asked Lizzie, who was busy collating cheques.

'No, but I think the rest will have to wait until Monday. I keep making stupid mistakes.'

'Doing anything nice over the weekend?'

'Nothing special,' lied Chloe. 'How about you?'

'I wasn't, but that nice Iranian man, the friend of Carlos Rocca, has invited me to his garden party tomorrow. I'm really excited about it. I bet his house is gorgeous. He told me that he holds a garden party every year, always for charity, and this year the proceeds will come to us. Isn't that great news?'

Chloe felt as though someone had punched her in the solar plexus. 'Yes,' she said weakly.

Lizzie laughed. 'You could sound more enthusiastic. We're talking thousands of pounds here. Why don't you come along with me? I'm sure he wouldn't mind. After all, he only got to hear of us through you. To be honest, I'm surprised he hasn't invited you anyway. I imagined that the two of you must be quite close, considering the size of that donation he gave because of you.'

'I haven't seen him lately,' said Chloe, realising that for once she was telling the truth.

'Well, he does have a wife. Maybe it's better that way. Would you like to come with me?'

'Sorry, I can't,' muttered Chloe.

'Why not? You said you weren't doing anything special.'

'I'd rather not, okay?'

Lizzie looked taken aback. 'I didn't realise he was a sensitive subject. I'll tell you all about it on Monday. I'm quite sure it isn't going to be anything like other garden parties I've been to!'

Chloe felt sick. 'I'm sure you're right. Look, is it okay if I go now? I've got a bit of a headache coming on.'

Lizzie looked across at her. 'You are rather pale. That's fine, you get off home. Try and get some rest before Monday too, you look exhausted.'

By the time she got home, Chloe was seething with anger. 'Where's Senhor Rocca?' she asked Mrs Clarke.

163

'He's gone out,' replied the housekeeper.

'Out where?'

Obviously taken aback by her tone, the woman looked apologetic. 'He didn't tell me. I'm sorry.'

'Did he at least say when he'd be back?'

'Late, he won't be eating dinner here.'

'Damn!' snapped Chloe, going into the drawing room and throwing her handbag on to the sofa.

'Temper, temper!' murmured Livia. 'What's the matter with you? A hard day at the office?'

'No. Work's easy, it's my social life that's becoming difficult.'

Livia's eyes sparkled. 'Carlos is rather hard to keep up with. Innocent young girls like you really shouldn't try.'

'He didn't give me a lot of choice. I was caught in his net before I realised what was happening to me.'

'Really?' asked Livia, disbelief clear in her voice. 'You mean you haven't enjoyed yourself so far? In that case, you should have a career on the stage. As far as I can see, you've taken to your new life like a duck to water.'

'Well you should know, you're always around.'

Livia smiled, getting up from her chair and gliding across the room to pour herself a drink. 'Does that annoy you? Carlos likes to have me around when he's training you. I understand the rules, you see.'

'It's a pity Mehrdad doesn't understand them better,' said Chloe bitterly.

Livia stood very still. 'Meaning what?'

'I shall talk to Carlos about it when he gets back.'

'Tell me,' suggested the Brazilian girl. 'I'll pass the message on, I promise.'

Looking at the tall, bronzed beauty, Chloe knew better than to trust her. 'I'd prefer to do it personally. Now if you'll excuse me, I need to shower and change before dinner. Do you know when Carlos is due back?'

'About eleven.'

'Fine, I'll talk to him then.' With that, Chloe left Livia and went upstairs.

Over dinner that night, Livia kept trying to find out what it was that Chloe wanted to discuss with Carlos, but still Chloe refused to tell her. By the end of the meal, the atmosphere between the two young women was very strained, and Chloe was relieved when Livia drove away from the house only minutes after she'd finished her coffee.

When Carlos finally did return, it was nearly eleven-thirty and there was still no sign of Livia. 'I thought you'd be in bed,' he said to Chloe when he found her curled up in Livia's chair in the drawing room.

'I waited up to talk to you.'

His eyes swept over her, and she became acutely aware that the scooped neckline of her dress revealed the soft swell of her breasts. 'I'm glad you did,' he said with a smile. 'Have you ever thought of pinning your hair up?' he added, crossing the room and running his fingers through her tousled dark curls. 'There, that looks wonderful. Perhaps you should have it up tomorrow afternoon.'

Chloe's eyes had closed as his fingers moved through her hair, but now they flew open. 'I don't think I can go ahead with tomorrow afternoon. Mehrdad has invited Lizzie, my boss. That wasn't part of the agreement. You promised me that no one I knew would be there.'

Carlos frowned. 'Are you sure of this?'

'Of course I'm sure. Lizzie told me herself.'

'You have to go. I've told Mehrdad it will be you. Besides, you gave me your word.'

Chloe laughed bitterly. 'It doesn't seem that a person's word counts for much round here.'

Carlos glared at her. 'My word is important to me. I would never lie to you over something like that. I'll tell Mehrdad that Lizzie must be kept away from the marquee, and that the pair of you cannot meet up. Does that satisfy you?'

'Is that a promise?' asked Chloe.

'Yes, it is. I give you my word on it. You have to trust me, I've told you that before. Mehrdad will never go against my wishes; he can't afford to upset me.'

It was obvious that Carlos meant what he was saying, that his word was sacred to him, and despite her misgivings, Chloe knew that she must accept his assurances. 'All right,' she conceded reluctantly. 'But please ring him now.' Carlos nodded and walked away to his study and his private phone.

Neither he nor Chloe noticed that during the course of their conversation Livia had returned, and had been standing in the hallway listening to every word.

'Here we are,' said Carlos cheerfully, bringing the car to a halt outside Mehrdad's Hampstead home. 'It looks as though some people are already here. I think we should take you in through the side entrance, Chloe. No one should see you before you're in your costume.'

Chloe, whose mouth was dry with nerves, felt her stomach tighten. 'What do you mean, costume?'

'You have to look right for the exhibition. Don't worry, Mehrdad has excellent taste. Livia, take Chloe round the side of the house while I go and tell them that she's here. It's a beautiful day for this, I must say.'

Chloe wasn't in any mood to appreciate the warm summer sunshine or the cloudless sky. She thought that she would have preferred it to be raining, that way there would almost certainly have been fewer visitors. As it was,

166

she had a feeling that everyone who'd been invited would turn up, and that would include Lizzie.

As she walked in through the kitchen door and stood shivering in the cool of the kitchen itself, Mehrdad came in from a door on the opposite side of the room. He smiled at her. 'How wonderful to see you, Chloe. I was afraid you'd change your mind, although Carlos said you were very eager to help make today a success. I'll take you upstairs and you can get changed. Livia, Carlos said to tell you that he'd meet you in the herb garden.'

Livia gave him a warm, sensuous smile and nodded. She then gave Chloe a quick, indifferent glance. 'Good luck,' she said briefly, and with a thin smile she was gone.

'Would you mind undressing for me?' asked Mehrdad politely once they were upstairs, as though the two of them had never shared the intimacy of the night of Carlos's dinner.

'What do I have to wear?' asked Chloe nervously.

'Nothing extreme. Did Carlos explain the rules of the game to you?'

'He hasn't really told me anything about it.'

'It's quite simple. You masturbate yourself to orgasm three times in the first half-hour, which means that anyone who's interested will have a chance to see what makes you come before the competition gets under way in earnest. After that, you have a brief break and then anyone who wants to touch you pays fifty pounds to charity. If they manage to bring you to orgasm in ten minutes, they win a small prize. The person who extracts the final orgasm from you wins a crate of champagne and has the opportunity of meeting you again at your charity's dinner.'

Chloe stared at him in disbelief. 'What if I don't want to meet that person again?'

Now it was Mehrdad's turn to show surprise. 'Carlos said that you'd be happy to go along with this. He'll be

167

with you when you meet up with the winner, so you'll be quite safe.'

'I find that very little consolation,' she retorted. 'I'm sorry, Mehrdad, but that's not acceptable to me. I can't just arrange to meet a stranger for sex, which is presumably what will be expected at some stage of the evening.'

Mehrdad raised his eyebrows. 'Isn't that what you did with Rob?'

She felt as though he'd slapped her round the face. 'How do you know about Rob?' she whispered. 'Even Carlos doesn't know about him.'

'Chloe, you must try and understand that it isn't possible to keep secrets from Carlos. Of course he knows about Rob. He has you followed wherever you go. How else can he keep control of you? He is meant to be in control of you, isn't he? I understood that was the agreement between the two of you.'

'Not exactly. Did he set Rob up for me?' she added, as she stepped into a short white tunic dress with thin shoulder straps that was only just long enough to cover her buttocks.

'No. When he talked to me about it, he was quite angry. Here, turn around, I want to put your mask on.'

Chloe began to back away. 'I don't think I want to wear a mask.'

'It will add to the air of mystery, make it more exciting for everyone. Also, it helps to conceal your true identity. Fiona is going to put your hair up as well, as an additional disguise.'

His words reminded Chloe about Lizzie. 'Has Carlos told you that I don't want Lizzie seeing me in the marquee?' she asked urgently.

Mehrdad nodded. 'Yes, and I'm sorry that I didn't realise it would be awkward for you when I invited her. Don't worry, I will make certain that she stays away.'

'She wouldn't be interested in this sort of thing,' explained Chloe, 'but it could cost me my job.'

'You're worth far too much to her charity for that to happen,' said Fiona, hurrying into the room. 'Quickly, let me get your hair done. Lots of people are arriving, and we need to get you in place. You look wonderful like that,' she added.

Mehrdad sat Chloe down on a stool in front of a full-length mirror, so that she could see herself as Fiona worked on her. The simple pure white dress gave her an almost virginal air of innocence, which was in sharp contrast to the white leather mask, with holes for her eyes, that covered the top half of her face.

Once Fiona had pinned Chloe's dark curls up in a sophisticated style, the contrast was even more extraordinary, but Mehrdad had one more finishing touch to add. Carefully he placed a thin black leather collar around her neck, with a leash attached. As soon as it was fastened, he tugged gently on it, pulling her upwards until she was standing.

She stared at her reflection, unable to believe what she was seeing. She was a bizarre and arousing mixture of innocence and sexuality, dark and light, and as Mehrdad stood close behind her she could tell that he was already aroused.

'Time to go,' he said huskily, and suddenly she realised that there was no turning back. The moment she'd been both dreading and anticipating for over a week had finally arrived.

CHAPTER

19

Mehrdad walked ahead of her all the way to the marquee, keeping the leash taut. When he went out through the front door, and she saw all the people walking around on the front lawn, Chloe tried to pull back.

Immediately Mehrdad tugged sharply on the leash, and she was jerked forward. 'Keep your head up high,' he whispered. 'Walk proudly, show them that you're not ashamed of your body.'

Still Chloe hesitated, her head down as her cheeks flushed with embarrassment. Then, out of the corner of her eye, she caught sight of Carlos watching her, with Livia standing beside him. The Brazilian girl was smiling, and whispering in her lover's ear. Chloe knew that it was important she didn't let Carlos down, that she must show him she could be disciplined.

Following Mehrdad round the side of the house and into the marquee at the far end of the enormous back garden, she kept her head high and didn't look at anyone, concentrating on the feel of the grass beneath her bare feet.

Once inside the tent, she was taken to a raised platform which had an old-fashioned chaise-longue on it, with a tiny pillow at one end. On the floor next to it, she saw some small glass bottles. As Mehrdad signalled for her to sit down, he looped the end of her leash over a hook set in the back of the chaise-longue. 'The bottles contain oils and creams that you might want to help you masturbate,' he explained quietly. Then, without another word, he left her.

Although she was now sitting on the chaise-longue, the leash was long enough to allow her to lie down if she wanted to. Looking about her, and letting her eyes adjust to the relative gloom compared with the bright sunlight outside, she saw that there were already about twenty people in the marquee with her.

It was eerily quiet. A few of the men and women were whispering to one another, but most of them were silent, their gaze fixed on the masked Chloe. She remained sitting, her knees primly together like a schoolgirl's, and she could feel herself trembling. She didn't know how to begin.

After a few more minutes, the people in the tent became restless, and started to murmur amongst themselves. Still Chloe sat there. She wanted to begin, to start pleasuring herself, but it was impossible. Then, as she was about to speak, to call out to the onlookers that she wasn't going to go through with it, she saw Carlos come into the tent.

His bright blue eyes pierced right through her, and she saw him give a small nod, like a secret signal between them. Immediately she felt better. He was there, watching her, supporting her, and she would show him how much he'd taught her and how well she'd learnt the lessons.

Slowly, sensuously, she slipped the straps of the white tunic off her shoulders, looking out over the heads of the watching people until she was staring directly at Carlos. Moistening her dry lips with the tip of her tongue, she then eased the dress down over her hips, and the audience responded with a soft sigh of excitement. Chloe's breathing

171

quickened and she wriggled her hips until the dress fell round her ankles. For a brief moment she waited, her gaze still locked on to Carlos, and then she stepped out of the dress and kicked it off the platform. Two men scrambled to pick it up, and she felt a surge of power rush through her as she realised that it was the audience, not her, who were the true slaves.

Reaching down, she picked up a small bottle of scented massage oil and poured some into the palm of her left hand. Then she rubbed her hands together until her fingers were slippery and sensuous, before lying down on her back with her head resting on the small velvet pillow.

Lightly she stroked herself on her shoulders, arms and upper chest, but she deliberately avoided her breasts, and soon they started to ache with need. She'd forgotten the watchers now; all she was concentrating on was the image of Carlos staring at her, judging and assessing her actions and responses.

After a time, when her nipples began to harden, she allowed her slippery fingers to caress the tiny buds, until they were rigid and tight. Her hands played with her breasts, then moved down the sides of her body and across her belly until she began to tremble with the onset of her first climax.

She could hear her own breathing quicken as she rolled her left nipple between the thumb and finger of her right hand, and when she pinched it hard she gave a tiny cry of pain before her carefully tutored body responded with a short, sharp orgasm that made her hips jerk upwards.

Suddenly she heard people talking, their voices shrill and excited, and abruptly she remembered that she wasn't alone with Carlos; she was in front of a group of total strangers, who were paying to witness her pleasuring herself.

For a time she lay still, and the voices faded away as the tent emptied. Lifting her head, she saw that they had all gone except for Carlos, who was still standing by the entrance, watching her intently.

She stared back at him through the mask, wondering how he felt watching her like this, but then a new group of people started crowding into the tent and soon it was time for her to give herself her second orgasm.

This time she lay on her side, facing them all but with her eyes closed. For the first time she allowed her oiled fingers to move slowly and teasingly around the entrance to her vagina as she bent her top leg to give them all a better view. She didn't care about the watchers any more; it was all about her and Carlos. Her body's response was quick, and her clitoris swelled as she gently stroked the surrounding tissue in between sliding her middle finger in and out of herself.

As she felt a pulse start to throb behind her clitoris, she rolled on to her stomach, squeezing her thighs together tightly. This increased the delicious pressure that was building up inside her, and as her excitement grew she started to writhe frantically on the chaise-longue.

Hot flickers of pleasure snaked through her, her fingers worked faster and faster and her whole body grew tight. She was nearly there now, and when she lightly touched the side of the stem of her clitoris she felt her muscles bunch together in a spasm of ecstasy. 'Yes!' she cried in delight, and then her orgasm flooded through her and she ground herself against the velvet covering beneath her.

This time the watchers took longer to leave, and she could feel their excitement filling the marquee. Finally, though, it was quiet, and opening her eyes she stared down the length of the tent to where Carlos was standing. He didn't seem to have moved a muscle, and his face was expressionless, but she knew the effect she was having on him and this exhilarated her.

By the time the marquee was full for the final time, Chloe was worried that she wouldn't be able to reach a third climax on her own. When she started to caress herself, her body seemed less responsive, and as she rolled on to her back she remembered what it had felt like when Carlos had taken her from behind, lunging into her rectum with such passionate intensity that the pain had seemed as nothing compared to the pleasure.

The memory was enough to excite her. Now, as she stroked her rounded breasts with one hand while caressing between her thighs with the other, every nerve ending responded immediately. Soon her body was climbing rapidly towards orgasm, and when she dipped her fingers into her own juices and spread them around the soft, delicate tissue of her inner sex lips, she started to moan out loud.

She felt as though a hand was inside her, pulling all her muscles tightly upwards. Images of all the things that she'd done since meeting Carlos flashed through her mind, and with startling speed her pleasure peaked and she cried out at the intensity of the pleasure that swamped her.

For several minutes she continued to groan and whimper, her fingers lightly touching her breasts as she savoured the last dying flickers of her climax, but finally it ended and she forced herself to be still.

Lying with her eyes closed, she was vaguely aware that it was taking even longer for the marquee to empty this time, and the sound of the audience's excited voices lasted a long time, but finally there was silence. Slowly she opened her eyes, and it was only then that she realised Carlos was standing over her.

'You seemed to enjoy yourself,' he said quietly.

Chloe nodded. 'In a strange way, I did. It was exciting. I felt different, as though I was controlling them.'

Carlos looked amused. 'You *were* controlling them. You played them very well. Even I was impressed. I told you that through discipline comes a kind of freedom, but that's something you have to experience for yourself before you can understand it.'

'I don't know how I'll feel now, when strangers start touching me,' she confessed.

'You must enjoy yourself, take the pleasure that they give you and revel in it. Allow it to flood through you, savour every moment. Remember, they are the ones on trial. They have to show that they can arouse you as well as you can arouse yourself. Quite a daunting prospect after the demonstration you've given them!'

'Mehrdad says that they've each got ten minutes,' explained Chloe. 'I hope there aren't too many of them. I shall be exhausted.'

He shook his head. 'That won't happen. Once you're tired you'll cease to reach a climax and then the show is over.'

'The last person to satisfy me is coming to the charity dinner with our group. What if I don't like them?'

'Why should you dislike them? If they can give you sexual satisfaction, what could there be to object to?'

'Lots of things, I imagine. I don't know. I haven't thought it through, but—'

Carlos laid a finger against her lips. 'Hush! It's time for the second part of the competition. Relax and enjoy it. You mustn't worry about things you can't control.'

'Will you stay here all the time?' asked Chloe.

'Most of the time. I must go and find Livia now, while Mehrdad prepares you. So far, I've been very proud of you. Don't disappoint me at this stage.'

Before Chloe could reply, Carlos had gone, and Mehrdad was climbing on to the platform while two men lifted a strange wooden contraption on to the front of it for him to position.

Sitting upright, Chloe felt the collar round her neck tighten. The leash was stopping her from moving forward as far as she wanted to go. As she made a small sound of frustration, Mehrdad looked round at her. 'Don't worry, this isn't as fearsome as it looks. It's to make things easier for you and the contestants.'

'What is it?' asked Chloe nervously, thinking that it looked rather like an old-fashioned set of stocks, but built for two people rather than one.

When Mehrdad had finished fastening it to the platform floor, he caught hold of the end of Chloe's leash and led her over to it, forcing her right up close.

As her breasts squashed against the framework, she realised why the contraption had two holes, but before she had time to protest, Mehrdad had forced each of her softly rounded globes through them and then rested her chin in a groove on the top of the framework. Next he spread her legs apart, and looping two chains round her ankles, fastened them to the floor. Finally he pulled her hands behind her back and cuffed them, so that her breasts jutted through the two holes even more proudly.

Moving round in front of Chloe, Mehrdad examined her carefully. There was a small wooden stool to the side of him, and pulling it across, he sat down on it. Immediately his face was level with Chloe's imprisoned breasts. He touched the tips lightly before starting to caress her belly and upper thighs.

'That seems about right,' he remarked. 'The stocks reach just below your breasts, which means that all your erogenous zones are accessible to the competitors. With your legs spread like that it's perfect. I hope you're not uncomfortable,' he added as an afterthought.

'No, not really, but I feel very exposed,' said Chloe nervously.

'That's the whole idea. You have to be exposed, otherwise how can the competitors bring you to orgasm?'

'But I feel too vulnerable, it's frightening,' whispered Chloe.

Mehrdad gave her a gentle smile. 'You're meant to feel frightened, Chloe. It's what Carlos wanted. He said that it would add an extra dimension to your excitement.'

'I don't need an extra dimension. Please, can't I just lie on the chaise-longue, like I did for the first part?' begged Chloe, who was starting to tremble with fear.

Ruefully, Mehrdad shook his head. 'I'm afraid not. Carlos has approved this, and anyway it's time for the competition to begin. All the tickets have sold out, the marquee will be packed. This is definitely going to be remembered as the best garden party I've ever given.'

'You will keep Lizzie away, won't you?' Chloe reminded him.

'Of course. Don't worry. Livia has offered to look after her for me. Now I must go, everyone will be getting impatient.'

'No, not Livia!' shouted Chloe, but it was too late. Mehrdad was out of earshot and people were already filing into the marquee.

Before the marquee flaps were closed, Chloe noticed that outside the sun was still shining brightly. Inside, though, it was almost dark. Just as her eyes started to adjust to the gloom, a spotlight blazed directly on to her, and she was briefly blinded. Even when she was able to see again, it was impossible for her to make out individual faces in the crowd. This meant that she could no longer draw comfort from Carlos's presence.

As the first competitor came on to the platform, Mehrdad put what looked like a giant hourglass on the makeshift stage. 'Once you begin, I shall start the timer,' he explained to the waiting man. 'The sand takes ten minutes to run through. If you've succeeded in bringing her to orgasm by then, you win a small prize. If not, at least you know you've contributed to a charitable cause. There are no losers in this game, except possibly Chloe,' he added with a smile.

Chloe looked at the man taking his seat on the stool in front of her. He was in his mid-thirties, fair-haired, slim, and very expensively dressed. As his hands began to fondle her breasts, he looked at Chloe with naked desire in his eyes, and she was immediately aroused by his excitement.

It was soon clear to her that he'd watched carefully when she'd been masturbating, because he began to pinch her nipples between finger and thumb, waiting until she winced with pain before releasing them. Then he licked them with long, rough strokes of his tongue while his hands strayed over her belly and thighs before parting her sex lips and stroking her rapidly hardening clitoris.

He was so deft, so assured and skilful, that Chloe quickly felt her body growing hot, and all too soon her muscles tightened and she shook from head to toe as an orgasm rippled through her. With a brief, admiring smile the man took his prize from Mehrdad and then reluctantly left the platform.

He was followed by a dark-haired woman, who knelt between Chloe's outspread legs and brought her to a climax very quickly, using only her tongue. Then an older man also won a prize by inserting his tongue deep inside Chloe and pressing the tip against her G-spot.

By now the atmosphere in the marquee was charged with sexual excitement. Every time that Chloe climaxed she uttered tiny cries of satisfaction, and her pleasure only served to increase the arousal of the watchers in the shadows as they waited their turn to bring her to a peak of ecstasy.

The atmosphere helped Chloe. She knew that Carlos was watching her, and that he would be pleased with the way she was responding to the sheer hedonistic pleasure of it all. However, by the time the eighth competitor was sitting on the stool, Chloe was beginning to tire. He tried everything he could think of, licking and sucking on her breasts and thrusting his fingers inside her damp vagina, but it seemed to take an age before she felt the first tell-tale flickers of an impending climax, and after she'd come she saw that the sand had nearly run through the timer.

Slumping against the wooden frame, she wondered who the next competitor would be, because she had a feeling that this one might be the last to satisfy her and so would win a place at the charity dinner with Carlos and his friends.

As he walked on to the platform, the man looked straight into Chloe's eyes, and she felt a sudden, startling jolt of recognition. It wasn't that she'd met him before, but she could tell that he understood her and that, like Carlos, he knew exactly how to please her. He and Carlos were two of a kind, she realised, and it amazed her. She'd imagined that Carlos was unique.

Sitting on the stool, he rested his hands on each side of her waist, and then remained perfectly still as she waited tensely for him to make a move. Her flesh began to twitch and her legs to shake, but despite the fact that the timer had been set in motion, he still did nothing.

His hands seemed to be burning against her skin. She longed for him to touch her somewhere else, to caress her throbbing breasts or trail his fingers between her burning thighs, but all he did was sit and watch her until she let out a whimper of despair.

Then, with a sudden swift movement, his left hand caught hold of her right breast and she felt him gripping the nipple tightly between his fingers, while his right hand moved between her outspread legs. She was so frantic with need that she thrust her pelvis forward to assist him, and then gasped as he slapped her lower belly hard with the back of his hand. 'Keep still,' he instructed her, his voice low but clear. Chloe knew that she must obey, because this was a man she wanted to meet again, but it was hard as he teased her velvety flesh, circling but never touching her aching clitoris.

She could hear her breathing growing heavy, and knew that it must be carrying through the marquee, but she didn't care, because the dark, dangerous desire was building up inside her, and she knew that this man could satisfy it, just as Carlos could.

Soon she was soaking wet between her thighs, and she thought that the man would now use his tongue on her, but instead he got up and moved the stool so that he was sitting behind her. Chloe tensed, knowing what was coming, dreading it and yet desiring it too.

Gently, almost tenderly, he parted her buttocks and reaching between her legs dipped his fingers in her juices and spread them between her buttocks before waiting for an agonising second. Then, as Chloe's belly tightened painfully, he thrust two fingers deep inside her rectum, while at the same time the fingers of his other hand finally caressed her swollen clitoris.

She felt a leaping flame of red-hot pain course through her entire body, quickly followed by an explosion of liquid heat between her thighs, and as the two contrasting sensations joined together she was racked by one of the most intense climaxes she'd ever experienced and screamed in an ecstasy of pain-filled pleasure.

The stranger reached round her from behind, and his hands remained on her breasts until her body was completely still. 'Don't climax again today,' he whispered against her ear. 'I want to win and join you at the dinner. I must see you again. I need to talk to you.' Chloe didn't turn her head, didn't acknowledge his words in any way, but she knew that he was confident she would make sure his instruction was obeyed. She knew too that she mustn't let Carlos know.

The next competitor was a beautiful young woman of about Chloe's own age. She strode confidently on to the platform, and smiled at Chloe. 'I'm Louise, and I want to go to that dinner with Carlos,' she whispered, sitting on the stool that was once more in front of Chloe. 'I know you're tired, but I'm sure I can bring you to orgasm just one more time.'

Chloe wasn't bothered by Louise's words. She felt certain that her body was too exhausted to respond any more, but as her breasts were gently stroked and kneaded, and her nipples hardened, she realised that she could be wrong. The trouble was that she was still thinking about the intriguing stranger, and as a result was aroused.

When Louise closed her mouth around Chloe's left nipple and nipped at the tight little peak with her teeth, Chloe found herself imagining that it was the stranger still pleasuring her, and tiny flickers of arousal began to dart through her. Frantically she fought to subdue them, but then Louise trailed her fingers down over Chloe's hipbones and stroked the creases at the top of her thighs, and she felt herself begin to shiver with rising pleasure.

She wanted to scream in protest, to stop her overexcited body from responding, but then Louise opened up Chloe's outer sex lips and began to suck lightly on the exposed little nub that was pulsating with need. Chloe's breath snagged, and Louise gave a tiny laugh of satisfaction.

Chloe felt her stomach muscles starting to tighten, her hips jerked and her legs shook with tension as her climax grew inexorably nearer. There was nothing she could do to prevent it now, not with Louise's clever mouth working its magic between her thighs, but just as she was resigned to losing her private battle, there was a disturbance at the entrance to the marquee.

Although Louise didn't stop what she was doing, Chloe looked out over the watching crowd and saw Livia walking in, accompanied by Lizzie. As Lizzie looked down the length of the marquee she seemed to stare directly into her eyes, and the effect on Chloe was instantaneous. The erotic spell was completely broken as she froze in horror, aware that her worst nightmare had come true.

She was vaguely aware that Louise still had her head between her thighs, but it had no effect on her at all, and she knew that thanks to Livia the moment of danger had passed.

'Time, I'm afraid,' called Mehrdad from the shadows.

Louise lifted her head and turned to face him. 'That wasn't fair. She was distracted.'

'It was your responsibility to keep her interested!' laughed Mehrdad. 'Come on, Louise. It was only a game. It's all in a good cause, remember?'

Sullenly, Louise left the platform, and then Mehrdad unfastened Chloe and, taking the leash in his left hand, led her down through the watching people, who parted to let her pass. Some of them clapped; others simply watched with fascination as she kept her head high.

It was only when she reached the entrance to the marquee and saw Lizzie, who was standing with Livia and

Carlos, looking at her in incredulous disbelief, that embarrassment swamped Chloe as she finally realised what she'd done. Suddenly she longed for the safety of the house, and she quickened her steps.

At last, after what seemed the longest walk of her life, she was finally back in the bedroom, where she found Fiona waiting to help her shower and change.

CHAPTER

20

'What did you feel like?' asked Fiona half an hour later, as Chloe stood looking out of the bedroom window.

Chloe thought for a moment. 'Initially I was frightened, but once it all started I felt strangely powerful.'

Fiona frowned. 'You were on a leash, nothing more than a plaything, how could you feel powerful?'

'I think it was because I realised that I was controlling their emotions. Without me there, there was nothing. I was the catalyst for all the excitement, and it was my sexuality which turned them on. You'd have to experience it to know what I mean.'

'No thank you,' said Fiona with a shiver. 'I'd die of embarrassment. I'm all for experimentation, but not in front of an audience that size. Who won, do you know?'

This was the question that Chloe wanted answered, but she decided to feign indifference. 'No idea. It was a man, that's all I can remember.'

'It was Taylor Woods,' said Mehrdad, coming into the room.

'Who's Taylor Woods?' asked Chloe, as Fiona gave an excited squeal.

'A wealthy businessman who has quite a reputation with

the ladies. Carlos doesn't like him very much. He won't be pleased to learn that it's Taylor joining us for the dinner. He'll have to take Mike's place.'

'I didn't know you'd invited Taylor here today,' remarked Fiona.

'I didn't,' said Mehrdad. 'I suppose one of the women must have brought him along as her partner.'

Chloe decided to risk a question. 'Will he fit in with us all?' she asked casually.

'He'll fit in with the ladies, that's for sure. Carlos doesn't like him because they're alike in many ways: self-contained and difficult to get to know. I doubt if he's got much small talk.'

Fiona giggled. 'It's not his small talk that the girls enjoy! What was he like today, Chloe? You must remember!'

'I don't,' said Chloe, who could actually remember every detail of the way he'd brought her to orgasm. 'He can't have been that special.'

'He won, that makes him quite special,' Mehrdad pointed out.

'He only won because you didn't keep your word and Lizzie came into the marquee,' retorted Chloe. 'If I hadn't been distracted by her, that blond girl might have won. She was very good. I can remember her.'

Mehrdad looked very uncomfortable. 'I'm really sorry about Lizzie. Livia must have thought the competition was over. Carlos is furious.'

'Not as furious as I am. Carlos doesn't have to go in to work and face her on Monday. I do,' Chloe pointed out. 'Now, if you don't mind, I'd like to go home.'

'Carlos thought you'd want to leave. He's waiting for you in the car at the front of the house,' said Mehrdad. 'Fiona and I look forward to seeing you at the dinner. It should be a wonderful evening.'

185

'I'm not quite sure what to expect,' confessed Chloe.

Fiona kissed her on the cheek before showing her down the stairs and out through the front door. 'Expect the unexpected,' she said softly.

'What do you mean?' asked Chloe, but Fiona refused to say any more. She simply smiled and said goodbye before closing the door firmly behind the departing Chloe.

Carlos was already in the driving seat as Chloe got into the car. He glanced sideways at her. 'I'm sorry that Lizzie somehow managed to get into the marquee. It was unforgivable, and Livia will be punished for it.'

'I just hope it hasn't cost me my job,' said Chloe furiously. 'What am I meant to say to her on Monday morning? Have you any idea what I felt like when I saw her there? It was—'

'It helped to make sure that Taylor joined us for the dinner,' said Carlos smoothly.

Chloe tensed nervously. 'Who?' she asked innocently.

'Taylor Woods, the man who won the competition.'

'And is it a good thing that he won, or a bad thing?'

Carlos took a corner too fast and swore under his breath. 'From your point of view I'd say that it was a good thing. You enjoyed him pleasuring you, I could tell.'

'I enjoyed everyone pleasuring me. I thought that was the idea of it all. You told me to enjoy it, and I did.'

'Taylor was different from the others,' he replied tersely.

'He didn't seem different to me.'

'You should know better by now than to lie to me, Chloe. I know you better than you know yourself. He spoke to you too. What did he say?'

'He spoke so quietly I couldn't hear,' said Chloe. Then, aware that Carlos was in a dangerous mood, she decided to go on the attack, something she'd never done before. 'I don't know what's the matter with you,' she continued

186

angrily. 'I thought that I'd done well, and you'd be happy. I really tried to please you, to do all the things you said, and I thought I'd succeeded, but you're not pleased at all. In fact, you seem angry with me. Why? What did I do wrong?'

She saw Carlos's hands relax their grip a little on the steering wheel. 'You didn't do anything wrong,' he said after a brief silence. 'You were wonderful. You exceeded my greatest expectations, and I was truly proud of you. I apologise. I'm annoyed with Livia because through her, I broke my promise to you. Stupidly, I'm letting that annoyance spill over on to you.

'The control you displayed this afternoon was incredible. You've nearly mastered the discipline now, there is very little left for you to learn. Soon, after the dinner, you will have completed your apprenticeship with me. Then we must decide what the future holds for you.'

'I can't believe what happened myself,' confessed Chloe. 'As to the future, perhaps there will be things that you demand of me at the dinner that I can't do. I could still fail you.'

'I don't think it's likely,' said Carlos smoothly.

'No,' confessed Chloe. 'After this afternoon, neither do I, but I suppose it's still possible.'

'Oh yes,' said Carlos with a slight smile. 'It's definitely still possible. Here we are, safely home. You go in and rest. I have to go back for Livia. We won't be home until late. Mehrdad and Fiona have invited us to stay for dinner. Tomorrow I have to go to a business meeting all day, so I won't see you before you go back to work. I wish you luck for your meeting with Lizzie.'

'I'll need all the luck I can get,' remarked Chloe, getting out of the car. At the front door she turned to wave goodbye to Carlos, but he was already driving away and she was irrationally disappointed. For a few minutes it had seemed that she really mattered to him, that he was capable of a more normal relationship with her, but now she wasn't so sure.

Although Chloe got in to work early on the Monday morning, Lizzie had arrived before her and was sitting behind her desk.

'Morning,' said Chloe casually, but Lizzie didn't answer. Hoping that if she just kept her head down and got on with her work, nothing more would be said, Chloe began to sort through the morning's post.

After a long silence, Lizzie turned and looked at her. 'I'm surprised you had the nerve to come in this morning after what I saw at the weekend.'

'What's that got to do with my working here?' demanded Chloe.

'Quite a lot, since I understand that you claimed to be making such a disgusting exhibition of yourself on behalf of this charity. I don't think I've ever been so shocked in my entire life as I was when I walked into that tent. I recognised you immediately, despite that stupid mask. It was disgraceful. You looked like some girl in a sleazy nightclub in Soho. Heaven only knows what the nuns in Rio would have thought if they could have seen you. You used this charity as an excuse for a perverted, lewd exhibition and—'

'That's enough,' said Chloe sharply. 'I'm sorry you didn't like what you saw. The show wasn't intended to be open to everyone, only a selected few. Livia made a mistake when she brought you in, but—'

'You're the one who made a mistake,' retorted Lizzie. 'I still can't believe what I saw. You're here this morning, little Miss Prim as usual, and yet when you were up on that stage you were behaving like a cheap whore.'

Chloe took a deep breath. 'I'm sorry you feel that way

about it, Lizzie. I did it for a reason that I can't even begin to explain to you, but I don't regret it. I don't consider I behaved like a whore, but even if I had, it certainly wasn't a cheap one! However, since you're so upset, I'll make sure that none of the money we raised comes to this charity. I'd hate you to feel that the street children were being helped by tainted money.'

Lizzie's cheeks were flushed, and she couldn't meet Chloe's eyes. 'I don't want Mehrdad to think I'm ungrateful,' she muttered. 'He was very sweet to me afterwards, and—'

'And doubtless told you exactly how much money he hoped to be able to give you,' said Chloe sharply.

'He did mention a sum. It was very large. I realise that things probably got out of hand, and it certainly wasn't his fault, so I shall accept his cheque. The problem is, Chloe . . .'

Chloe looked at her one-time friend in disgust. 'You're no better than the nuns were,' she said slowly. 'Well, I hope you do accept the money, but don't be fooled by Mehrdad's charming manner. Believe me, he's no sexual innocent. He's more decadent than you could begin to imagine.'

'Even if that's true, it's different for men,' replied Lizzie.

'That's a ridiculous thing to say, but I don't want to get into an argument because there's no point. Obviously the show was a shock to you and I'm sorry. I'm not sorry that I did it, but I'm sorry that you saw it.'

'How could you do it?' asked Lizzie. 'How could you stand up there in front of all those people and let strangers touch you in such an intimate way? Don't you have any shame?'

'No one was hurt,' replied Chloe. 'It was just a bit of fun. Where was the harm in it?'

'What about your self-respect? Don't you realise what men think about women who behave like that?'

'There's a whole world out there that you don't know anything about, Lizzie,' said Chloe quietly. 'I didn't know about it either, until I met Carlos Rocca. Now that I do know, I understand that it's a world that suits me, and believe it or not, it's a way of life that's going to set me free.'

'You didn't look very free to me, standing there like some slave girl in olden times while all the men fantasised about you,' snapped Lizzie.

Chloe realised that, in a way, Lizzie was jealous of what she'd witnessed, and she suspected that this jealousy was going to make it difficult for them to continue working alongside each other for much longer.

'Since you're going to take the money that was raised, I think we'd better agree not to talk about this any more,' she said firmly. 'As soon as the gala dinner is over, I'll look for another job.'

'I think that's an excellent idea,' said Lizzie stiffly. 'I'm sure you understand why I feel the way I do about it all.'

Chloe smiled to herself. 'Yes, I certainly do,' she agreed. The two women didn't speak again for the rest of the day.

The weeks leading up to the dinner passed very slowly for Chloe. The atmosphere at work wasn't good, and although no one said anything, she had a suspicion that Lizzie must have told most of the other people at work about what she'd seen at Mehrdad's garden party. Certainly no one was very friendly towards her any more, and she kept searching through the evening paper for jobs that would suit her, but with no success.

'I don't know why you're doing that,' remarked Carlos one evening, when he came across her sitting at the kitchen table with the paper spread out in front of her.

'Because I can't stay where I am for much longer, thanks to Livia,' snapped Chloe.

Carlos nodded sympathetically. 'I realise how difficult she's made life for you, and she's been punished, but you don't need to think about another job. Soon I'll want you to be my English hostess, looking after this house and helping me entertain my guests. It will be a full-time position.'

'But Livia does that.'

'Perhaps, once you've completely mastered the discipline, Livia will not be needed here. She could return to my house in Rio, or possibly find herself a new life. You don't yet understand the plans that I have for you if all goes well at the dinner,' he added, stroking the back of her neck.

Chloe trembled with pleasure. Recently Carlos had been away a lot, and she was frantic for the heights of physical ecstasy that he enabled her to reach. Just thinking about the things he did to her aroused her, and her rigid nipples brushed against the thin silk of her blouse.

'Are you missing me?' he whispered, reaching round her and lightly caressing the tight little buds through the material. Chloe nodded. 'That's good. I want you to be needy for the dinner party. I want you frantic to be pleasured, desperate for sexual release. It's all part of the training. Famine followed by feast is a highly rewarding experience.'

His fingers tightened round her left nipple and she gasped as a sharp pain lanced through her breast. He continued to grip the aching tip, pinching it even harder until she cried out with pain. Roughly he pulled her chair round until she was facing him, then tore her blouse open and closed his mouth around the abused nipple.

She felt his tongue flicking tenderly at the throbbing flesh, but then his teeth started to close around it and she tensed, waiting for the next wave of pain. As he bit slowly down on the nipple she arched her back as the pain deepened, causing her whole body to explode into a shamefully quick and intense orgasm.

'Very good,' he murmured. 'You've learnt well. No more now, not until the night of the dinner. I've selected a dress for you to wear then, and just before we leave I'll also tell you exactly what you have to do during the evening in order to complete the discipline. Think of it as your graduation night.'

Cupping her aching breast in her hand, Chloe longed for the waiting to be over.

CHAPTER

21

As Chloe looked at herself in the mirror for a final check, she hoped that Carlos would be satisfied with her appearance now that the big night had finally arrived. The dress, which had been delivered that afternoon, was dark red and black. The strapless red bodice fitted tightly, emphasising her gently rounded breasts, and the split at the front of the flared full-length black-and-red skirt nearly reached the top of her hold-up stockings.

His instructions to her had been clear. It had to be easy for her to be sexually available during the evening, which meant that she wasn't wearing any underwear beneath the exotic dress. Apart from that, she still didn't know what he expected of her during her final test.

As she turned to go downstairs, Carlos came into the bedroom. His piercing blue eyes narrowed as he studied her intently. 'Excellent,' he said at last. 'I can hardly keep my hands off you myself. The car's here, I just have time to tell you the rules for tonight, and then we must leave.

'I've decided against the anal plug. Instead I've set you three tasks. If you succeed in them, then you will have completed the discipline. First, you must bring one of the other girls in our party to orgasm during the pre-dinner drinks—'

'But that's not possible!' exclaimed Chloe. 'How can I do that when—'

'Second,' he continued, ignoring the interruption, 'you must experience two orgasms yourself during the dinner. Third, we will have a private auction at our table, with sealed bids. You will fulfil the sexual fantasy of the winner.'

'And what happens if I succeed?' she asked.

He gave her one of his rare smiles, and her stomach lurched with desire. 'Why, then Livia returns to Rio, you will act as my hostess here and the game will begin again, with a new apprentice.'

Chloe frowned. 'That would mean that if the new apprentice succeeded, I'd be like Livia, and find myself cast off.'

'You're being ridiculously melodramatic, Chloe. Come along, everyone is downstairs waiting. I do hope you weren't expecting some kind of conventional ending to your sexual apprenticeship; that would be very boring.'

'I was hoping for something rather more exciting,' said Chloe sharply, and had the satisfaction of seeing an expression of surprise cross Carlos's face as she swept out of the room.

Livia, Fiona, Mehrdad and Taylor Woods were all waiting in the drawing room, and when she joined them, Taylor's eyes gleamed with appreciation. He was tall and well built, with a mass of thick steel-grey hair and dark-brown eyes. 'You look very lovely tonight,' he murmured, as Carlos helped her on with her wrap. She smiled at him.

'The others have gone on ahead,' Livia explained to her lover. 'I told Chris that we'd meet up with them in the bar.'

'Excellent,' said Carlos approvingly. 'Chloe, everyone at our table knows what you have to do tonight, and I'm sure they'll all be eager to help you succeed. Now we must leave; we don't want to be late and annoy Lizzie again!'

'I wish Livia had never annoyed her in the first place,' muttered Chloe, but Livia only laughed. Then Carlos put an arm round his mistress's waist and soon they were all getting into the chauffeur-driven limousine that was waiting at the front of the house.

'By the end of the night, you'll know how well you've learnt all the lessons of the past months,' said Mehrdad. 'Are you excited?'

'No, I'm nervous,' replied Chloe, and it was true. The palms of her hands felt damp and her mouth was dry. In order to do all that Carlos was demanding of her, Chloe was going to have to take tremendous risks. The prospect of the humiliation that might lie in store for her was almost as bad as the prospect of failing and being rejected from Carlos's world of darkly bizarre sexuality, a world that she now needed as much as she needed food and drink.

When they arrived at the hotel, it was Taylor who helped her out of the car and escorted her into the bar, where the others were waiting for them. 'Good luck,' he whispered, and then he disappeared into the centre of the group. A few minutes later she was standing with a vodka and tonic in her hand, wondering how she could possibly have sex with another woman at a time like this.

'Hi,' said Natasha, coming over and smiling brightly at Chloe. 'I hear I missed a treat at Mehrdad's garden party!'

'Yes, you did,' agreed Chloe, her mind racing as she searched for a solution to her problem. 'You don't know where the loo is, do you?' she added.

'Sure, you go outside, turn left and it's about five doors down on your right.'

Chloe sighed. 'Would you mind showing me? I always get lost in hotels, and I'm a bit nervous tonight as it is.'

'I'm not surprised,' said Natasha sympathetically. 'Come on then, follow me.'

As Chloe followed her she knew that this would be her only chance, and that she had to take advantage of it. If she failed, then it would all be over before the night had even begun.

'Here you are,' said Natasha, pushing open the door to the ladies' loo. 'Think you can find your own way back?'

Chloe touched Natasha's arm. 'Come in with me,' she murmured. 'You won't regret it.' Natasha's green eyes widened and then, after a moment's hesitation, she smiled and followed Chloe into the ladies' cloakroom.

There were two other women standing in front of the basins, but Chloe ignored them. Pushing open the door to one of the cubicles, she pulled Natasha inside with her, and then locked it. Natasha stood with her back against the door, breathing heavily as she waited for Chloe's next move.

As Natasha was wearing a full-length dress, Chloe realised that it was going to be difficult for her to do what Carlos wanted, but it was obvious that Natasha was aroused, and when Chloe crouched down, the auburn-haired girl smiled and quickly lifted her skirt to make it easy for her.

Kneeling on the floor, Chloe ran her hands up Natasha's legs until her fingers touched the bare flesh at the top of her stockings. Gently she caressed the silken skin, and then, when she moved her hands higher, she realised that Natasha wasn't wearing any panties. Quickly she parted the other girl's sex lips and ran her tongue slowly back and forth over the moist flesh, lingering over the tiny swollen clitoris for a few fleeting seconds before moving on.

Natasha's breath caught in her throat. Her head went back and she started to whimper softly with pleasure. Remembering how Livia had caressed and aroused the red-head, Chloe redoubled her efforts, and soon Natasha's legs were trembling and her whole body grew tense.

Aware that she was running out of time, Chloe drew the other girl's sex lips even further apart, and then inserted the tip of her tongue deep inside her until she was whimpering with delight. With teasing slowness, Chloe began to draw Natasha's clitoris into her mouth, sucking gently at first but then more firmly before releasing it and running her tongue down the side of the shaft.

'Yes, God, yes!' moaned Natasha, thrusting her hips forward.

Chloe could imagine the tiny tingling sensations that must be spreading through Natasha's body, and how tight and tense she must feel as her climax approached. Now she used more pressure as she flicked her tongue rapidly up and down the stem of the clitoris for a few more seconds before moving it with tantalising tenderness back and forth over the sensitive head.

With a sharp cry of ecstasy, Natasha climaxed, her hips jerking forward and her pelvis arching towards Chloe as the pleasure flooded through it. When she'd finished, Chloe continued to stimulate her, and although she made token sounds of protest, within a few seconds Natasha was once more flooded by an orgasm of almost painfully exquisite ecstasy.

It was only the sound of voices outside the cubicle door that made Chloe stop. She'd been relishing every moment of Natasha's orgasms, and enjoying too the sensation of power that the moment was giving her. It was with a sense of regret that she stood up, and when she looked into the other woman's green eyes she knew that the regret was mutual.

A few minutes later they both emerged into the cloak-room, and ignoring the stunned and disapproving glances of the other women who were there, they tidied themselves up and then returned to the bar.

'Can we ever meet up on our own?' Natasha whispered to Chloe as Carlos approached them, but Chloe shook her head. It was something that she would have liked as well, but she couldn't imagine Carlos allowing it, and for the first time she felt a tiny flash of resentment towards him.

'Well?' he asked, handing her a fresh vodka and tonic.

'Mission accomplished,' she said with a smile.

He kissed her lightly on the lips. 'I'm very pleased to hear it. Now we go in to eat. You will be sitting between Taylor and myself, with Mehrdad opposite you. The seating arrangements are significant, and should give you the best possible chance of meeting my demands for the evening.'

A few minutes later, they all moved towards the dining room, and Chloe, who'd been highly aroused by Natasha's excitement, felt a surge of excited anticipation run through her. It was only when they took their seats and she saw that Lizzie was also sitting at their table that she started to worry.

The long, narrow top table was on a raised dais at the end of the dining room. It was covered by a thick white damask cloth, but the cloth only reached just below the table edge and Chloe realised that people sitting at the tables on the floor of the room would be able to see anything that happened. To make matters worse, Rob was in charge of their table. He gave Chloe a brief but unmistakably familiar smile, bringing back memories of Richmond Park.

She was seated between Carlos and Taylor, facing out towards the other diners. Mehrdad was opposite her, with Fiona on his left and Natasha on his right. Christopher was on the other side of Natasha, and next to him was an unsmiling Lizzie. Livia was sitting next to the chairman, Sir Lionel French.

Chloe was too tense to enjoy the first course of salmon and watercress mousse, because she knew that soon one of the men was going to make a move. After Rob had served her with the main course, just as Taylor had asked her what she'd been doing in Rio when she met Carlos, she felt someone's foot moving slowly up between her legs.

Startled, she looked across the table. When Mehrdad smiled innocently at her she knew for certain that it was him. He'd obviously slipped his foot out of his shoe and sock, and now he wriggled his toes against the soft flesh of her inner thighs, while Taylor waited patiently for her reply.

'I was a . . .' She stopped as Mehrdad's toes began to press firmly and insistently against her vulva, making her wriggle on her seat.

'Yes?' enquired Taylor politely.

'A nun,' she gasped, feeling her sex lips swelling and parting as the delicious stimulation continued. Hot tingles spread through her pelvic area, and without thinking she slid lower in her seat, trying to make her clitoris available to him. Then, ashamed of herself, she straightened up again.

'Remember, you have to come twice during the meal,' Carlos whispered in her ear. Hastily she lowered herself again, and this time Mehrdad's foot moved deftly so that his big toe was stimulating the hot, throbbing collection of nerve endings that was aching with desire.

'You didn't look like a nun in the marquee,' commented Taylor drily.

Chloe was so busy trying to suppress her whimpers of excitement that she couldn't answer him. She could feel perspiration breaking out on her top lip, and as she lifted her fork to her mouth, her hand trembled.

'Are you all right, Chloe?' asked Lizzie suddenly.

'Fine, thank you,' she said politely, and then gasped as she felt the big toe sliding inside her, moving around in tiny circles.

Taylor looked at her in apparent concern. 'Is the beef tough?'

'No, it's perfect, absolutely perfect,' she gabbled. Mehrdad was now sliding his toes up and down the damp channel between her sex lips, occasionally caressing her clitoris as he did so, but never for long enough to allow her to climax.

She knew that her breasts were swelling, could feel them pressing against the tight top of her dress, and it felt as though she was on fire between her thighs. Struggling to continue talking to Taylor, and desperate not to attract more unwanted attention from Lizzie or Rob, she still wanted to feel the delicious flooding pleasure race through her, and moved her hips forward.

'Chloe, is your chair uncomfortable?' asked Lizzie. 'You seem to be slipping off it.'

'No, it's fine,' she replied, and then, as Mehrdad gently moved his toes against the side of her clitoris while pressing against the whole vulva with the soft pad beneath his big toe, she gave a tiny cry as she was abruptly swamped by a series of sharp muscular contractions and a delicious orgasm washed over her.

By now nearly everyone at the table was looking at her, and quite a lot of the people sitting beneath them too. One man, who'd clearly seen everything that had happened, was staring at her with an expression of undisguised lust.

'Well done,' murmured Carlos. 'I think that we'd better wait until dessert before we try to help you with your second, don't you?'

Chloe nodded, ashamed and yet exhilarated. When she finally turned to look at Taylor again she realised that he knew what had happened, and that he was highly aroused by the knowledge.

'When do we make our sealed bids for your special raffle prize?' he asked Carlos.

'What special raffle prize?' asked Lizzie.

'Chloe has kindly agreed to help the winner of my private raffle to fulfil his or her greatest sexual fantasy,' explained Carlos.

Chloe winced at the expression on Lizzie's face. 'Did you have to tell her?' she hissed angrily.

Carlos shook his head. 'No, I didn't have to, but it amused me to do so just the same.'

Taylor leant across in front of her and passed an envelope to Carlos. 'My bid,' he explained.

Carlos looked thoughtfully at him. 'You're in quite a hurry, Taylor. Anyone would think this was a business takeover, not an intriguing diversion.'

By the time the main course was cleared away, Carlos had a pile of sealed bids in front of him. 'Aren't you going to bid?' asked Chloe.

'Of course not. Tonight I'm here to observe, to make sure that you obey me down to the last detail. You and I will celebrate later, when you've passed with flying colours.'

She was disappointed, but as Rob and his waiters moved round the table with the individual crème brulées, she distracted herself by wondering how she was going to be brought to her second and final orgasm during the meal. She didn't have to wait long to find out.

'Chloe, tell everyone here about our first meeting,' Carlos ordered her as she picked up her spoon. 'It's a subject that interests them all.'

Surprised by the request, she began to speak, and at the same time she felt his left hand sliding over her lap and then in through the deep split in the skirt until he was stroking her pubic hair. Lightly he tugged on the crisp curls, and then he pressed down hard against the flesh at the top of the hair, arousing a dull ache deep inside her.

She began to talk faster, trying to get her story finished

before she climaxed, but Mehrdad kept interrupting her with questions, and all the time Carlos's fingers were moving with diabolical skill over her frantic, slippery flesh. He teased and tormented her, pinching her clitoris lightly between two outspread fingers until she felt a pulse starting to beat behind it, then releasing her so that the throbbing stopped and her pleasure was thwarted.

Chloe could hear herself gabbling now, tripping over her words as she lost concentration because of the way her body was responding to Carlos's skilful ministrations. When he slid two fingers deep inside her and pressed against her vaginal walls she moaned in ecstasy, and while most of the people round the table smiled knowingly, Lizzie glared furiously at her.

'I'm sorry,' she muttered. 'I think I've got a trapped nerve.'

'Do go on with your story,' said Taylor. 'You were telling us how Carlos opened your eyes to the truth about the nuns.'

'He opened my eyes to the truth about a lot of things,' she said huskily, and then, as he nipped her clitoris sharply between his finger and thumb and began to squeeze hard, tears of pain welled up in her eyes and her voice faltered.

'You were saying?' said Natasha sweetly.

Carlos continued to squeeze harder, and as pain threatened to overwhelm her, Chloe lost control. 'Oh God, it's no good. I can't concentrate. It's too much, please . . .' she gasped.

As everyone stared at her, Carlos finally relented and gently stroked one finger over the entrance to her urethra. All the incredibly intense sensations joined together and her desperate, well-trained body spasmed in a pain-racked climax that seemed all the sweeter because of what had gone before.

When the last ripples had died away, Chloe sank into her seat, breathless, exhausted and ashamed, but above all triumphant. Her ordeal was nearly over. Soon she would have completed the discipline, and in the process discovered more about her own sexuality than she would have believed possible.

Carlos gave her knee a squeeze and then removed his hand from beneath the tablecloth. 'So, it seems that I opened your eyes to the truth about human nature, Chloe,' he remarked, picking up on what she'd been trying to say. 'Do you think I did you a favour?'

'Yes, you did,' she said breathlessly.

'I wonder if that's true,' mused Taylor. 'I mean, did you really open her eyes to the truth about all human nature, Carlos? Your own, for instance?'

'I think Chloe understands me very well,' retorted Carlos smoothly.

Taylor smiled thinly. 'I hope so. When will you be opening the sealed bids?'

'During the speeches.'

Chloe was relieved that she was going to have a brief respite, but anxious to find out who'd won the auction. She hoped it wasn't Livia, because she felt certain that she wouldn't enjoy bringing her greatest sexual fantasy to life.

Eventually, after the coffee and mints were cleared away and Rob had left with one final backward glance, the speeches began. Just before Lizzie got to her feet, Carlos opened all the envelopes, then, looking over to Livia, he shrugged, as though absolving himself of all responsibility for the result.

'Taylor, you're the winner,' he announced. 'It's a very high bid, most charitable of you. I've no doubt that you have a very fertile imagination, so Chloe should have an interesting time.'

Chloe turned her head and looked into Taylor's eyes.

They were almost as unfathomable as Carlos's, but not as hard. 'Yes, I think it will be interesting for her,' he replied, and at that moment Lizzie rose to her feet to speak.

As she started to thank everyone for making the evening such a success, Taylor stood up, drawing Chloe to her feet as well. Then, ignoring what was happening around them, he pushed her back over the damask-covered table before peeling the top of her dress down over her breasts until they were totally exposed.

Lizzie had her back to them, and didn't seem to hear the sudden intake of breath from the assembled guests as she launched into her well-rehearsed speech.

Chloe couldn't believe what was happening. In front of everyone, Taylor's hands were fondling her nipples and stroking her upper body as he prepared to enter her, watched by over a hundred people, and because she so desperately wanted to succeed in completing the discipline, she didn't dare try to stop him. This was his fantasy, and she had to make it come true for him.

She didn't expect her body to respond, didn't imagine that it could under the circumstances, but when she felt his massive erection probing the entrance to her vagina she was suddenly consumed with desire to feel him inside her, to be filled and satisfied in full view of everyone there.

As he thrust himself into her, Taylor rested his hands on the table each side of her body, and then rotated his hips in tiny circular movements that immediately stimulated her nerve endings, making her belly tighten and her breathing quicken.

'When you come, you must scream loudly,' he whispered. 'I want them all to hear when your pleasure spills.'

Chloe stared at him in horror, her lips forming the word 'no'.

'That's my fantasy, and I paid a lot of money to make it

come true,' he reminded her as he continued to move around inside her.

Her body was responding rapidly now. It felt as though coiled snakes were slithering and sliding deep inside her belly, and she longed for the moment when the rapidly mounting tension dissipated in a rush of liquid heat, but the sound of Lizzie's voice was a distraction and she stayed balanced on the edge of her climax, unable to relax enough to come.

Realising that she was having difficulty, Taylor lowered himself on to her, then grasped her left nipple in his right hand and flicked hard at the end of the tight little peak. Her nipple started to sting and burn, and her whole breast throbbed. The nipple seemed to be joined to a tiny cord that ended behind her clitoris, and the cord tugged at all the clamouring nerve endings that were bunched together there. In a frantic rush, her hips rose and then she was coming and coming, screaming with pleasure and relief as she realised that she'd finally completed the discipline.

She was vaguely aware that Lizzie had stopped speaking, and that there was chaos in the room, but she didn't care. Even when Taylor pulled her up, put his jacket round her and bundled her out into the corridor, away from the lascivious gaze of the other guests, she didn't feel embarrassed. All she could think about was that she'd succeeded.

Eventually Taylor found a small deserted room and helped Chloe into a chair. 'Are you all right?' he asked gently.

'I'm fine,' she said with a smile, but as she started to think about what she'd done, her body began to shake.

'You were incredible,' he said softly. 'I've never met a girl like you before, never. I didn't really expect you to do it, you know.'

Chloe stared at him in surprise. 'But I had to, you knew that. It was the last test. Now I've completed the discipline.'

He gave a short laugh. 'Of course, the discipline. Well, I consider myself a very lucky man to have had this opportunity. Do you know what happens now that you've done so well?'

'Not really,' she admitted. 'I think Carlos wants me to be his London hostess. Livia will return to Rio, and then he'd like me to help him instruct another novice, presumably taking Livia's role this time.'

'And is that what you want?' he asked.

Chloe considered his question carefully. 'Not really,' she admitted. 'For one thing, if the next novice succeeds, where does that leave me? Also, Carlos always said that through the discipline I'd become free. Well, he was right, I have become free, but now I'd like a chance to live my life using all the things I've learnt, but on my own terms. The trouble is, that's not possible.'

'Why not?' asked Taylor, straightening her dress and letting his hands linger on her bare shoulders as he spoke.

Chloe laughed. 'Because I need Carlos. I suppose that's the clever part of his discipline. He's taught me to enjoy the kind of pleasures that only he can provide.'

'I don't think that's true. I seemed to provide you with a reasonable amount of pleasure tonight, and I'd be delighted to do the same again another time. There are a lot of men and women who enjoy the dark and dangerous kind of sexuality that Carlos has shown you.'

'Well I've never met them, except through Carlos,' retorted Chloe.

'But you could meet them. I'd help you. I have plenty of friends who share my sexual tastes, and yours too. Then there are the people you've met through Carlos, and each person you meet will know other like-minded people.

206

Think about that before you decide to stay with Carlos. Here, take my card. If you want to talk more about this, call me. I believe in true sexual freedom, and that includes independence.'

'But . . .'

Before Chloe could finish, the light was switched on and Carlos stood framed in the doorway. 'Here you are, Chloe! For a moment I thought you'd run away. Well done! You clearly made Taylor a very happy man, and most of the other male guests too, I suspect. Thank you for looking after her, Taylor, but I'll take over now.'

Taylor nodded. 'Of course, and don't forget what I said, Chloe. I meant it.'

Carlos watched Taylor thoughtfully as he left them alone together. 'What precisely did he mean?'

'That I'd made his most secret fantasy come true and he would always be grateful,' she lied.

'Is that all he said?'

'Yes, why?'

'No special reason. He seemed a little too possessive of you for my liking, that's all. Come along then, Chloe. It's time for us to go home and celebrate.'

When she awoke the next morning, Chloe could hardly move. Every muscle in her body ached, and her breasts, vagina and rectum were sore and throbbing. In spite of that she felt marvellous. During the night Carlos had brought her to peaks of incredible ecstasy, combined with moments of exquisitely dark pain that had only served to heighten the pleasure.

Now, lying sprawled in the middle of his vast bed, she could hardly believe the things that they'd done, but when she ran her hands over her sore body the memories flooded back in full, and she knew that it was all true.

Next to her, Carlos stirred, throwing an arm over her in his sleep. For a few minutes she savoured their physical closeness, but then his eyes opened and he moved his arm. 'Quite a night,' he said sleepily. 'I'm looking forward to the next few months.'

Chloe didn't reply, and later, after they'd both showered and dressed, he raised the subject again. 'Are you excited about the future, Chloe?' he asked, his expression making it plain that he was in no doubt as to what her reply would be.

She thought for a moment. 'I'm not sure.'

He frowned. 'What do you mean, not sure? Are you tired of England? We could leave Livia here, and go to Rio. It would be easy to find an innocent young girl there, maybe even another novice from a religious order! Teaching sensual but unawakened girls about our world is more exciting than you can imagine, especially when they struggle to suppress their true sexuality.'

As he was talking, Chloe knew for certain that this wasn't what she wanted, and she felt a sharp stab of sadness because by teaching her so much, Carlos had actually driven her away from him. 'I'm sorry, but I can't do that,' she said slowly.

He looked stunned. 'Why not?'

'I need to be free. You told me that through sexual discipline I'd become free, and it's true. I do feel free, which is why I can't stay with you any longer.'

'I don't understand,' said Carlos, his blue eyes puzzled.

'Because you always have to be in control, to keep your women obedient. Then, when you tire of them, you discard them. You're about to discard Livia, even though you pretend that you're not. What will happen to her when she's alone in Rio?'

He shrugged. 'That's not my responsibility. She's a mature woman and—'

'Yes, but she's dependent on you because that's the way you've shaped her sexuality. I don't want that to happen to me. I want to choose my own partners, and the way I want to be satisfied.'

Carlos shook his head. 'No you don't. You need to be disciplined and restrained in order to get total pleasure. I've made sure of that.'

'That's probably true, but I want it to be on my terms. There are men I like that you would never allow me to go with, like Rob and Taylor. They would both satisfy me in their different ways, and they have feelings too. I need feelings as well, Carlos, but I don't think you have any.'

Carlos looked sharply at her, his eyes turning cold. 'You're quite determined about this, aren't you? Did Taylor put the idea into your head?'

'No, I thought it out for myself. I do have a mind as well as a body, Carlos.'

'Indeed you do, which is one of the things I found so fascinating about you. However, it seems that I misjudged you badly. I rarely make mistakes, Chloe, but when I do I like to put them behind me as quickly as possible. I'm sure you can find somewhere else to go by tonight.'

'Tonight?' gasped Chloe in horror.

Carlos nodded. 'Yes, tonight. If you remain here, then I won't be answerable for what happens. However, I can tell you that it would make last night seem like a class for sexual beginners.'

Chloe realised that she'd hurt him badly, and that he was finding it hard to come to terms with her refusal, but she knew that he was speaking the truth when he said that she must leave at once.

'I'm sorry,' she said quietly. 'I shall miss you. I'd like you to come and see me once I've found somewhere to live, because I do need you, but I know that I can't stay with you for ever. You talk about freedom, yet you don't really want your women to be free. If you did, you'd understand why I'm doing this.'

'Well, I don't understand,' he said shortly. 'I'm going out. When I return this evening I don't want to find a single trace of you in this house.'

Chloe took a step towards him. 'Please, Carlos, tell me that you'll get back in touch one day, that we can stay friends. But for you I would never have learnt the truth about myself. You've done so much for me and—'

'You're a fool,' he snapped. 'God knows what will become of you when you leave here, but I imagine that in a few months' time you'll be living off charity yourself, rather than raising money for it in your truly unique way. Unfortunately, I doubt if Lizzie will have any sympathy for your plight, not after the way you behaved at, or should I say on, the dinner table last night.'

With that he walked out of the bedroom, leaving Chloe feeling horribly empty and bereft. Eventually she found the card that Taylor Woods had given her and then hurried to her bedroom to make a telephone call. Even though she would miss Carlos dreadfully, and this wasn't how she'd wanted their relationship to end, she knew that she was doing the right thing.

CHAPTER

22

In the basement of a three-storey town house in central London a man lay tethered face down on a circular bed, moaning softly as Chloe, sitting across the backs of his thighs, eased a large dildo into his back passage and then switched it on so that it vibrated vigorously.

Immediately his moans turned to cries of pain, cries which she ignored as she rocked back and forth in order to arouse herself. Finally, when her breathing grew rapid and her nipples hardened, she switched off the vibrator and then deftly released the man so that he could turn on to his back.

'You enjoyed that, Rob,' she said softly, looking down at his massive erection. 'Now you have to pleasure me, and don't come until I give you permission, or I shall have to really punish you.'

Rob swallowed nervously as she lowered herself on to him, and when she tightened her vaginal muscles around him she could tell that he was close to orgasm. 'Not yet,' she reminded him, feeling the first slivers of excitement darting through her. Carefully she released and contracted herself around his throbbing cock until he was crying out, begging her to let him come, but she was concentrating on her own pleasure.

Eventually, far too soon for her liking, her body was flooded with waves of ecstasy and her hips jerked as she threw her head back in delight. Beneath her, Rob lay motionless, frantically trying to control himself, and when she was still he breathed a sigh of relief.

'That was so good,' she murmured. 'Just one more for me, and then you can come too.'

Rob's eyes widened. 'I won't last,' he groaned.

Picking up a leather tawse from the bedside table, Chloe flicked it over his chest and belly until his skin turned red. 'I think you will,' she murmured, feeling him grow even harder inside her.

Swiftly she twisted herself round, so that she had her back to him, and then she watched herself in the full-length mirror at the end of the bed as she rode him relentlessly. She lifted herself up then lowered herself down, tightening her internal muscles around him and then releasing him, and her excitement was increased by his sobs of frustration as he struggled to subdue his own frantic need for satisfaction.

Finally she couldn't hold back her own orgasm any longer, and this time her body contracted sharply as the climax swept through her, making her groan with delight. When the very last tremors had died away, she swivelled round again, and looked down at Rob.

'You did very well,' she whispered, untying his hands. 'Now you can come.'

Immediately he reached up for her breasts, grasped them in his hands and roughly caressed them before grabbing her hips and lifting her up and down in short, rapid movements until, seconds later, his own pleasure finally spilled and he gave a loud shout of satisfaction.

About an hour later, as he was leaving, Rob looked

thoughtfully at Chloe. 'I often wonder if you can be as happy as I am,' he remarked.

'I'm happier than I ever believed possible,' she replied with a smile. 'I like my job, although advising charities on the best ways to raise money seems rather an ironic way for me to earn my living but they headhunted me. It seems that all publicity really is good publicity! Also, I love the life I have here. I was so lucky when Taylor offered to rent me this house, and for a ridiculously low amount too.'

Rob laughed. 'No doubt Taylor gains from the arrangement too.'

'Oh yes,' agreed Chloe with a smile. 'I think it suits both of us, and we see each other a lot.'

'No regrets then, about leaving Carlos?'

'None at all,' she said firmly as she showed him out. 'He seems a lifetime away.'

After she'd closed the door on Rob, she poured herself a vodka and tonic and thought about what he'd said. The truth of the matter was that she did miss Carlos. Through the various contacts she'd made during her time with him, she had a full and very active sex life but no one, not even Taylor, understood her deepest, darkest needs as well as Carlos.

Sometimes, in the small hours of the morning when she returned from a dinner out with Taylor, or a visit to the theatre with Rob, she would long to feel Carlos's hands hard on her breasts, and his teeth grazing her nipples, but despite this she was happy. She loved her freedom and the way she was now in control of her life. Brief moments of regret like that were, she supposed, a small price to pay in return.

When the doorbell rang she nearly didn't bother to answer it, but then, knowing that Taylor sometimes called in late, she changed her mind. 'I'm a bit tired,' she said, slipping off the safety chain.

213

'Why's that?' asked a familiar voice, and she found herself face to face with Carlos.

'What?' she asked stupidly.

'I wondered why you were tired. Don't bother to answer. I'm sure I can guess the answer. Are you going to ask me in?'

Her mouth had gone dry. 'Yes, sorry, of course. If I'd known you were coming I'd have—'

'I didn't know myself.' He looked directly at her for a moment, but then averted his eyes awkwardly. 'I've tried to put you out of my mind, Chloe, but it hasn't worked,' he admitted reluctantly. 'I found out from Mehrdad where you were living, and as I was passing I decided to take a chance that you might be in.'

'Well, you were right,' she said brightly, hoping that he couldn't see how her hands were shaking. 'How's Livia?'

'She's gone back to Brazil. She missed the sunshine.'

'Do you miss her?'

'Not particularly.'

'Was there anything special that you wanted to see me about?' asked Chloe.

'Yes,' he said quietly. 'I wanted to punish you for leaving me.'

Her heart began to race. 'I'm not sure that I . . .'

'Mehrdad said that you've got an interesting basement here. He described it very vividly to me. Perhaps we should talk further in there,' he suggested.

Chloe hesitated. She knew very well what would happen if she allowed him to go in there with her, and that if she let him back into her life there would be no turning back, but as her body began to throb and desire filled every atom of her being, she knew with absolute certainty that this was how she wanted it to be.

Slowly, trembling with excitement, she led him down

into the room that had been designed solely to gratify her desire for the perverse pleasures of the flesh that this man had taught her to enjoy. As he stood motionless, watching her intently, her stomach tightened with the familiar mixture of excitement and fear, and then he moved.

Catching hold of her shoulders, he tore off her clothes and pushed her roughly on to the bed, reaching for the handcuffs that were attached to the iron bedstead and imprisoning her wrists within seconds.

His hands were rough but clever, and soon she was moaning deliriously, caught up in the incredible excitement of having him tease and torment her frantic body once more. As he started to cover her tender nipples with the once-familiar cream that made her flesh throb and ache, intensifying all the sensations almost beyond endurance, she knew that the tables had now been completely turned.

Even as she heard herself crying out with the red-hot pain of exquisite sexual torment, her body more alive than it had been since she left him, she reminded herself that Carlos had been forced to come to her. What he was doing to her now was what she needed, what she enjoyed, and this time it was all on her terms.

Carlos really had liberated her, and at the same time he'd unwittingly enslaved himself. When he turned her on to her stomach and thrust himself hard inside the tender flesh of her rectum, sighing with pleasure as he did so, she realised that he knew it too.

The wheel had finally turned full circle, she thought, as her body rushed headlong into yet another orgasm. It was certainly not what he'd intended the discipline to accomplish, but from her point of view it was the perfect conclusion.